Lock Down Publications and Ca$h
Presents

IMMA DIE BOUT MINE

4

Heart of a Cannibal

By
Aryanna

First Edition 2024

Printed in the United States of America

This is a work of fiction. Names, characters, places, and incidents either are products of the author's imagination or are used fictitiously. Any similarity to actual events or locales or persons, living or dead, is entirely coincidental.

Lock Down Publications
P.O. Box 944
Stockbridge, GA 30281
www.lockdownpublications.com

Like our page on Facebook: Lock Down Publications
www.facebook.com/lockdownpublications.ldp

Stay Connected with Us!

Text **LOCKDOWN** to 22828 to stay up-to-date with new releases, sneak peaks, contests and more…

Like our page on Facebook:
Lock Down Publications

Join Lock Down Publications/The New Era Reading Group

Visit our website:
www.lockdownpublications.com

Follow us on Instagram:
Lock Down Publications

Email Us: We want to hear from you!

Chapter 1

(Tesha)

(Russia – Some Months Later)

The smell of garlic and onions snatched me from unconsciousness and brought me into the warmth of the kitchen where I could see good what was being prepared. Tynesha was chopping up carrots and tossing them into the baking pan along with red potatoes and the assortment of other fresh vegetables. The sounds of holiday music was playing somewhere in the background, which finally brought recognition and clarity to what I was seeing. This was the preparation for our Christmas dinner that me, Mom, and Ty always cooked together.

"Damn, bitch, are you gonna help me or just sit there? Since Mom is dead, I'mma need you to pick up the slack for this special occasion," Ty said, smiling at me as she stepped over to the oven to preheat it.

I moved to get up out of the chair that I was sitting in, but I immediately felt resistance in the form of zip ties biting into my wrists and ankles. When I looked down, I was horrified to see that I was naked, covered in blood, cuts, and bruises, even though I couldn't feel the pain.

"T-Ty, what is this? What's going on?" I asked, confused.

"It's Christmas dinner, dummy. What else would it be?"

"No, I mean why the fuck am I strapped to this goddamn chair, naked, and beat the fuck up?" I replied, working hard to control the hysteria within me.

"Oh, so you got amnesia now? I don't got time for the dumb shit, Tesha, and you're not a baby anymore, so I'm not holding your hand through this."

The feelings swirling inside me were more than confusion at this point but hearing the word 'baby' spoken aloud was like a gut punch that caused me to look down.

"My-My baby," I mumbled, looking at my body and realizing that I wasn't pregnant anymore.

"Don't worry, sis. Your baby girl is amazing, and I'll be getting her dressed in a few minutes. I just need to make sure this oven is preheated at 350°, and I gotta finish up these vegetables because our guests will be here before you know it."

"Cut me loose from this damn chair and I can help you after I get myself cleaned up," I said, trying again to pull my arms and legs away from the wooden chair.

"Don't worry about it, sis. I'll handle this. I can tell by the fact that you're asking questions about who did this to you and what happened that you're having another episode. That's okay because the doctor warned us that these types of things would happen, but I'm not gonna add to your stress levels by insisting that you help me with this last supper."

"But I-I want to help you, Ty! I'm not having any type of episode, and I know that I'm not crazy, so quit playing and cut me loose from this damn chair," I demanded, feeling anger take the place of fear.

"Bitch, who are you talking to like that? I'm here doing your ungrateful, undeserving ass a favor by cooking this feast, so I'mma need you to watch your fucking tone before I cut your tongue out and add it to the broth! The nerve of Judas catching a goddamn attitude," she said, shaking her head in disbelief while tossing more carrots into the pan.

"Judas? Who the fuck are you calling Judas, bitch?! Let me out of this muthafuckin chair and I'll show your ass what Judas can do to your holier than thou face!"

"Oh, I'm sorry, sis. Did me calling you Judas hit a nerve and offend you? Pardon me, maybe I should've just called you Fredo from the movie, *The Godfather*, since you betray family for your own selfish interests," she said, pointing at me with the sharp knife in her hand.

"Betray my family? Bitch, what the fuck are you babbling about?! I would never betray my family, and you know that shit."

"Really?" she asked, cocking her head to the side while staring at me with an evil glint in her hazel green eyes.

We were twins, so I knew that look she'd turned on me in an intimate way, and I knew it signaled a lie that she was prepared to hop on with proof of deception. I didn't say anything, but I did test the strength of my restraints again in hopes that I could free myself to fight whatever her devious mind was concocting. Her sudden sweet smile that she turned on me as she put the knife down inspired another shot of fear to shoot through my veins like adrenaline, increasing my anxiety. When she bent down, out of sight, behind the kitchen island in front of her that held the makings of dinner, I thought for a brief second that she was picking up a gun to shoot me, but then, I heard the soft cooing of a baby. When Ty reappeared, she was holding a naked baby girl in her arms, and it only took a glance for me to know that this was my daughter.

"Ty-Tynesha, what are you doing? What are you doing with Stormy?" I asked.

"Stormy? Is that what you and my husband decided to name your beautiful little bastard child?"

The words that sprang to my lips immediately were a quick denial of who my child's father was, followed by a promise to beat my sister's ass for calling my baby a bastard.

I said nothing though as my mind scrambled over the fact that Ty obviously knew about me and David having sex, which explained why she accused me of betrayal.

"Ty, I'm sorry. I'm so sorry, and I mean that from the bottom of my heart because I never meant to hurt you."

"You didn't? So, did you think that fucking my husband would make me feel some type of orgasmic pleasure because you and I are twins? That must be some new type of scientific shit because, on my life, I have never heard that shit right there," she said, looking over the top of Stormy's head at me.

"No, I didn't think no dumb shit like that. I just-I didn't think about anything, okay? I didn't fucking think, and I'm sorry!"

"It's okay, sis. I forgive you," she replied, kissing the top of Stormy's head.

"Y-You do? You forgive me?"

"Of course I do, Tesha! You're my muthafuckin twin sister, bitch, my best friend in the world, and you know that I could never stay mad at you. Especially not over some dick, even if it is really good dick," she replied, giggling.

Her laughter made Stormy laugh too, and the sound was as melodic as wind chimes blowing in the breeze. For a moment, I felt my body go limp with relief, but the moment didn't last because I was quickly reminded that I was still strapped to a chair when I tried to move.

"Untie me and bring me my baby," I said, fighting to sound polite and not demanding.

"Nah, sis, just relax while I finish up supper."

I opened my mouth to argue with logic instead of using threats, but I never got to say a word because she did something that left me speechless. With all the gentleness that one would expect from someone holding an infant, she laid my daughter down in the baking pan amongst the red potatoes and vegetables.

"Ty, what-what the fuck are you doing?" I asked in a voice that I barely recognized as my own whisper.

"What's it look like? I'm getting her dressed, dummy."

As improbable as her explanation sounded, I still found myself looking around for what clothes she was about to put on my child. When she picked up an open can of lard, dipped her fingers in it, and started smearing it on Stormy's thigh, I felt my mouth drop open in horror. For a split second, my mind frantically denied what my eyes were seeing, but Ty's continuous motions made this reality impossible to deny.

"Tynesha, get the fuck away from my daughter!" I screamed, struggling with all my might to get free of the chair imprisoning me.

"Bitch, calm down. She's loving the feeling of this cold fat on her skin. Don't worry. I'm spreading it evenly so that she'll be a perfect shade of golden-brown light-skinnedness."

"Ty, I swear to fucking God, bitch, you better GET AWAY from my fucking child!" I screamed, still fighting valiantly to get free.

"What the hell is all that noise?" David asked, strolling into the kitchen like he had not a care in the world.

"David-David, get Stormy! Get her away from your crazy ass wife!" I yelled, tasting the salty tears running into my mouth.

"Ty, what are you doing?" David asked.

"Just preparing dinner, my husband. You know, doing my wifely duties," she replied.

"Oh, okay. Well, Tesha, just chill the fuck out and let her work," he said nonchalantly.

"Let her-Let her WORK? Nigga, have you lost your muthafuckin mind?! She's about to kill our daughter, David!"

"Technically, she's Royal's daughter because it's his name on her birth certificate. I have no claim or obligations to her, plus this was Ty's way of me making my betrayal up to her," he replied.

"Oh, my God, do you hear what the fuck you're saying, David? She's gonna kill our baby!" I yelled hysterically.

"David, why don't you go finish watching the NBA basketball game, and I'll call you when it's time to eat?" Ty suggested.

"Okay, bae," he replied, kissing Ty on the forehead and leaving the room.

"Tynesha, you can't do this. She's just a baby, and she's your niece! Please," I begged, crying uncontrollably.

"I hear you, sis. I really do, but she was born of your sin, and she must therefore atone for what you've done. David has accepted this reality, and in time, you will too."

My tears were pouring from my eyes so fast that I could barely see, but I was able to clearly make out Ty opening the oven and moving the pan with Stormy inside toward it. Using all of my weight, I rocked forward until the balls of my feet touched the cool linoleum of the kitchen floor, and then, I was awkwardly moving toward Ty. My progress was slow, and I almost fell twice, but I kept myself steady as I prepared to ram into her with my full body weight. As I rounded the kitchen counter, I saw the oven door slam closed, and I felt my heart crumble.

"No!" I screamed, launching myself at Ty.

Being off balance didn't allow me to correct or stop my forward progress to counter Ty's sidestep of evasion, which caused me to run into the oven. Before I could regain my footing, I felt something hit me with incredible force in the back of my head. The next thing I knew, the kitchen floor was rushing up at me. My face bounced off the linoleum, and I felt myself sliding back into unconsciousness. The last thing that I heard was the muffled screaming and crying of my beautiful baby girl, but I was helpless, and I knew it. I'd failed her, and her death would haunt me forever.

Chapter 2

(Royal)

The first scream brought me out of a dead sleep, causing my heart to hammer hard enough to shake my lungs with the vibration. By the second scream, I had my chrome and black Springfield .45 in my right hand, and my eyes were scanning the darkness of my bedroom for the threat. The feeling of Tesha flailing wildly next to me, as if she were in a physical battle with a demon, quickly shifted my focus and helped me to understand what all the commotion was about. After returning my pistol to the nightstand, I wrapped my body around hers and put my mouth close to her ear.

"Baby, it's okay. You're okay. Just come back to me. Come back to me, T," I whispered lovingly.

She fought against me for a few more moments, and then, her body suddenly went limp in my arms. I could feel her heart still thumping like the piston in a race car engine, but I could tell by her breathing that she was awake now. It always took her a little while to pull herself back together after one of her night terrors, but I was always here for that part too. After time, she'd ceased to be embarrassed by these moments that she perceived as her own weakness, which made it easier for me to help her find her balance again. In the last year, her night terrors had steadily increased in both intensity and frequency, but we'd developed a system of aftercare for all of the different levels to this struggle. It took ten solid minutes of me cradling her before she tapped my forearm to let me know that it was okay to release her. Once I let her go, she headed for the bathroom while I went to Stormy's crib in the corner and checked on her. She was only three months old, but sleeping through the night wasn't an issue as long as she had on the customized noise cancellation headphones that we'd made for her. She was a good baby, a happy baby, and the love of my life next to her mother. Once I was sure that she wasn't about to wake up, I followed the sounds of running water into the bathroom where I stripped off my shorts and stepped into the shower with Tesha. She immediately handed me a bar of soap and a washcloth and turned her back to me. I lathered up the washcloth and then gently began to bathe her without saying a word or asking a question.

"It was bad, bae... really bad," she mumbled.

I could tell by the hitch in her voice that she was crying, but I knew that was exactly what she needed to do, so I just kept on washing her back.

"It was different this time though. This time, David was there, and-and he didn't do anything to save Stormy. He just... He let Ty put her in the oven and cook her to death," she said, sobbing.

Her revelation made my hand stop moving, and I pulled her body to mine again to give her the security she hadn't felt while she'd been asleep. Her night terrors varied in terms of the people involved and the setting, but they all ended the same, with her own twin sister murdering our baby in cold blood. We'd been to every doctor available, tried medications from different cultural backgrounds, but nothing had worked. At the rate shit was going, we were going to have to try some black magic though because I needed Tesha to know peace. I needed her to live without a paranoia so strong that she rarely ever left our thirty-room castle that I'd bought for her from a rich Russian oligarch. What was meant as a gift of promise and a home to call her own had turned into a fortress outside and a prison inside.

Everything in me wanted to single handedly change that for her, but I didn't know how, and that part made me the most frustrated. The fact that David had entered her night terrors only showed the progression into the darkness of her guilt for keeping her daughter away from him. I'd certainly hoped that decision wasn't one that would haunt her because it had been something that we'd agreed upon, but it would seem that I should've prayed instead of simply hoping.

"It's okay, baby. Nobody is gonna hurt Stormy. She has so many people already willing to die for her that she's more powerful than the president," I said truthfully.

"I know that she's protected and that she's a baby, so she hopefully won't remember my acting crazy, but Royal, what kind of life are we giving her if we keep her locked up inside this castle?"

"The life of a princess," I replied.

She turned around in my arms to face me and wrapped her arms around my neck.

"I'm being serious, bae. You know like I do that this isn't the life we envisioned for her or for us. If I wasn't so messed up..."

"Hush with all that, bae. You're not the issue, and I've told you that more times than I can count," I said, putting my index finger to her soft lips.

The war being waged within her revealed itself in the beauty of her eyes, and it was a battle that I'd come to know like the fingerprints on my hands. Despite all that had happened in terms of the family that Tesha had known no longer existing in her world, she didn't hate David or Ty enough to allow me to get rid of them. So, instead, I had to witness and endure the mental torture that them continuing to draw breath inflicted on the woman that I loved. Watching as this turned her into a shell of herself, my heart ached with a sense of helplessness, but my love for Tesha and Stormy remained unconditional, which meant that I would endure anything that I had to. No matter how bad I hurt in the process.

"Royal, I know that you would do anything for me, even if that means doing nothing except holding me. I love you more every day for that, more than you know."

"More than I know, huh? You wanna show me?" I asked, moving my hands to palm both of her ass cheeks and lifting her into the air.

Her smile was like morning sunshine parting the clouds, and it only intensified my hunger for her.

"What did you have in mind, handsome?"

"Well, I could tell you, or..."

I let the rest of my sentence dissolve in the kiss I initiated as I pinned her to the shower wall with the chiseled muscles of my chest. The intoxication of her lips and mouth made my new favorite flavor her morning breath, and I wasted no time guiding my throbbing dick up inside her as our kisses gave oxygen to our fire. Her pussy grip fought me like a welterweight champion, but after a few steady punches, we formed a partnership that was sure to ring a few bells. The feeling of her nails in my back, clenching and scratching every time I lifted up into her, tapped into the savage in me, which only made me fuck her harder. The quick rise of our body temperature only increased the steam surrounding us as the water bounced off our skin, creating a cocoon of heat. When her hands moved upwards into my shoulder length dreadlocks and she took a firm hold of them, I knew she was preparing to fuck me back, and I welcomed the challenge. The sudden sound of an alarm blaring loudly stopped my movements mid stroke, and before she could realize what was happening, I'd pulled my dick out of her and put her down.

"Stay here," I instructed, stepping out of the shower and pulling my shorts back on.

When I walked back into our bedroom, I paused long enough to grab my pistol, and then, I rushed out into the hallway to find the problem. I only made it halfway down the corridor before two of my men stepped out of the shadows by the top of the stairs.

"False alarm, sir. The perimeter is secure," Marko said in his crisp English accent.

"What triggered the alarm?" I asked.

"A pack of wolves triggered the motion sensors, but to be on the safe side, we sent a five-man team to look over the entirety of the outer compound," Emil replied.

I nodded in approval because that was exactly where my mind was going. Anytime there was a false alarm that was triggered, I always ordered it to be investigated thoroughly so that any weakness or oversight could be addressed immediately. Alarms didn't go off too often, but coincidence wasn't one of those things that I subscribed to, so the fact that Tesha's night terrors were getting worse was tickling the ends of my paranoia. I would move with more caution than ever now.

"Keep me updated," I said, turning to head back to the bedroom.

When I walked in the room, I could see Stormy moving around, trying to push the headphones off of her ears, but she wasn't fussing yet, so I left her alone and headed back toward the shower.

"Everything is good, T. It was a false..."

The sight of Tesha huddled on the shower floor, crying in the fetal position, stopped my heart faster than the scream had woken me up. My movement to her was fast, and I had her off the floor in my arms within seconds.

"It's okay, baby. It was just a false alarm," I said, trying to soothe her.

She clung to me, shaking in fear that absolutely destroyed my soul. No words came out of her mouth, but I didn't need her to verbalize the terror that she was feeling. I simply carried her back into the bedroom and laid her down in our bed. After running to the closet and grabbing her a towel, I returned to the bed and quickly dried her off from head to toe. By the time that was done, Stormy was fussing, so I picked her up and carried her back to the bed where I climbed in next to Tesha. Past experiences had taught me that the only thing Tesha loved more than me was our daughter and their bond, so it was my hope to surround her with enough love to counteract the trauma that I could still see. At first, she just laid there, but Stormy was having none of that, and she immediately started to climb on her mother's chest. I pulled the headphones off Stormy and laid back against my pillow while watching the most beautiful sight in the world. There was nothing like a mother's love. I knew that it was physically impossible for Tesha not to interact with her child, and sure enough, within seconds, they were laughing and exchanging baby talk. I waited a few minutes before I tried to slip out of bed, but Tesha's hand on my arm stopped me and forced me to look at her.

"I love you, bae."

"I know, and I love you too," I replied, smiling at her.

Her smile was warm and full of the love she declared, but I noticed a new shadow slide into her eyes that created a feeling of butterflies in me.

"We have enough money to travel the world nonstop, and still I know that I'd never feel as safe or content as I am in this moment. Your love and the love of our daughter sustains me, but now, I need to let it make me better. I need to trust you."

"I know that you trust me, T, so what are you talking about?" I asked, confused.

"I'm talking about trusting you to keep us safe... permanently."

I felt like I understood the words coming out of her mouth, but in no way did I want to misinterpret what she was saying to me.

"Sweetheart, I only know one way to make things safe permanently," I stated carefully.

"I understand that. My apprehension about that hasn't been about any love for David, and yes, I'll always love my twin on some level, but what's stopped me from courting their deaths is because this shit is my fault. I set all of this in motion by being on some hoe shit, and I own that fully, which is why I've hesitated to eliminate them, even though they're a threat. And honestly, they might not even be a threat anymore because we ain't heard shit from either of them in months now."

"Okay, so tell me exactly what you want, baby, and then, we can go from there. I'm behind you no matter what," I reassured her.

"I need to know if my sister and David actually pose a threat to our family or if this is all in my head because of guilt and the night terrors. I need to know if I'm crazy."

I could tell by the way that she looked at me as she made that last statement that this was the issue she needed addressed the most. She hadn't come straight out and told me before, but it was clear now that she was questioning her mental stability. I knew that no amount of positive word affirmations could change what her mind frame was at this point, so I kept my initial response to myself. Instead, I turned my mind to the task that she was asking me to complete.

"What happens if I feel like they're still a threat?" I asked calmly.

For a moment, she just stared at me with a blank stare, and then, her eyes focused on mine.

"If they pose a threat to us or our family, then you do what you gotta do. You kill 'em all, Royal. You kill everybody who could harm what we have."

Chapter 3

(David) (Ghana)

"Daddy, can I help feed Prince?" Dayjah asked, shaking me awake from my sleep.

"Huh?" I replied groggily.

"Let Daddy sleep, Dayjah. Yes, you can go help feed your little brother," Shaomi said from her prone position in my arms.

"Stay in bed with me," I whispered, tightening my grip on her as Dayjah scurried out of the room.

"I had no intentions on moving from this spot, which is why we have help to keep up with these energetic kids of yours."

"Are you sure that you want more some day?" I asked, kissing her neck in a soft, deliberate manner.

"Mmm, you know that I do, but you're not getting no pussy for another couple weeks, so get your hard dick from in between my legs."

"A couple weeks? Baby, our son is five weeks old already, and my dick is aching to be back up in your guts, so why the extra week?" I asked, gently rubbing her clit and leaving my dick right where it was.

"Because your impatient ass already popped my stitches once with that midnight quickie a week after Prince was born!" she replied, chuckling and scooting her lower body away from me.

17

I didn't feel discouraged because her movement only increased the pressure I was able to apply to her clit, and the sounds of her breathing changing was the beginning of a beautiful love song.

"I promise to go slow and be gentle," I whispered against her neck as my fingers continued their seductive walk.

"Y-You're lying, baby, now s-stop teasing me."

"I'm not lying, bae. I really will take my time and be gentle," I vowed, scooting right up on her so that she was once again feeling my dick like her own heartbeat.

"No-No pussy, David, please. You can get some ass though," she replied, moaning ever so slightly.

Her words came as a shock because she'd never given that part of herself to me or anyone else, but I wasn't about to argue. I quickly paused in what I was doing so that I could reach over to the nightstand and grab the bottle of warming lube that we kept for those marathon nights. Shaomi's pussy stayed wetter than every body of water on the planet, but this was new territory we were entering, and I wanted this experience to be pleasurable for both of us.

"Remember your promise, baby, and be gentle with me," she said, rolling over on her stomach and pulling the comforter back to expose her gorgeous naked body.

Seeing her like this never got old, especially since she had added fifteen pounds of hips and ass to her petite 5'1" frame. One hundred thirty pounds looked amazing on her and taming her curves had kept my athletic build in prime condition all year round. I made sure to close our bedroom door and lock it so that we wouldn't be interrupted, and then, I sprinted back to the bed.

"Just relax, Sha Sha. I got you."

"Don't got me, get me, and put that dick in me before I change my mind," she said, looking over her shoulder at me in a way that was breathtakingly sexy.

I wasted no time straddling her legs and squirting some of the lube into the crack of her ass, causing her to giggle. I made sure to massage the gel in and around her asshole until I was sure that I wouldn't inadvertently split her open, and then, I applied some all over my dick. The instant warmth had my eyes wide open and looking intently at her thick ass like a man who was famished from neglect. I consciously checked myself so that I would go slow, and then, I went for what I knew. The moment that the head of my dick was inside her, we both took a deep breath, and I froze right there for a few moments. Inch by inch, I descended into her until we were completely inseparable, and then, I pulled back out fast. My second stroke was given with the same care and patience, even though I could hear my knees knocking with the desire to run wild.

"Fuck," I moaned, pulling out of her slowly this time.

"I know. My shit is virgin tight, huh? Now make it all yours, baby," she purred, arching her back.

I needed no other invitation. I pushed back inside her until I was balls deep and lying flat on top of her. In that position, I placed my hands on top of hers and laced my fingers with hers while putting my lips right against her right ear lobe.

"I love you, baby," I whispered as I began feeding her long, slow strokes.

I was purposefully gentle until I felt her fucking me back, and then, I applied that pressure to my stroke that pinned her ass to the bed. I knew the sounds her body made better than anyone I'd ever been with, but the immediate escalation her climax took shocked me as much as it excited me. I knew what she needed in order to catch the wave she was chasing after, but I took my time pushing her to that limit. The length of my stroke shortened, and the pace quickened, forcing moans to roll off of her skilled tongue in a chorus to the harmony of our bodies colliding.

"Let-Let me," she demanded, trying to free her hands from mine.

"Patience, bae," I growled, tightening my grip on her fingers and fucking her harder.

I waited until the last possible moment, right before my own climax outran my control, and then, I reached under her body to rub her clit again. As soon as I touched her, a flash of light illuminated our room, and she came with a primal growl that beckoned to the animal in me. I came with her while steadily slamming my dick into her with enough force to shake the entire house, continuing until I was completely spent and gasping for air. After that, all I could do was lay there.

"Babe, damn, you not even gonna take the dick out of me?" she asked, chuckling.

I kissed her on the cheek before I rolled off and out of her.

"I'm not ashamed to say that your ass is better than any pussy I've ever had, except for yours."

"Aww, thanks, bae, but I know that you're just trying to gas me up so that I'll let you ride that ride again. Luckily for you, I enjoyed that shit as much as you did, and you kept your promise for the most part," she replied.

"What do you mean? I kept my promise completely."

"Yeah, until you lost your mind and you tried to push my colon out through my stomach," she said, laughing as she got up and went to the bathroom.

I started to get up and follow her, but the sound of knocking on our bedroom door shifted my focus. I hopped up and threw a pair of shorts on, expecting to find my daughter on the other side of the door, but instead, it was one of the housekeepers.

"What's wrong?" I asked immediately.

"Nothing, my king. I was sent to let you know that your uncle is waiting for you on the back veranda."

"Tell him I'll be right there," I said, closing the door and heading to my closet.

I grabbed a green, silk robe, and I put it on while stepping into a pair of matching cashmere slippers before I headed out the door. It was just after sunrise, and the beauty of the land surrounding our ancestral mansion was always especially mesmerizing in this moment. I ignored it for the most part though and focused on my uncle as I moved toward the table that he was sitting at.

"Good morning, Uncle Umar. How are you?" I asked, taking the seat opposite him.

"I have no complaints about life at the moment, nephew, but that only means I must be alert for the shadows that will surely darken our days to come."

"That sounds real ominous, Uncle. Are there any shadows in particular that we should be looking for?" I asked curiously.

He didn't immediately respond, instead turning his eyes out toward the beauty of the desert and the distant horizon. By now, I knew him well enough to know that I couldn't force a quick reply from his lips, nor should I try to. His wisdom was sage and unparalleled by anyone I'd ever had the privilege to know, and he'd graciously bestowed a lot of it on me in the last year. It was him who had quieted the bloodlust that had almost pushed me into a blind death match with Tynesha because my trust had gotten so bad that I'd been willing to kill her before she gave birth. His lessons on patience had become my religious zeal, and thankfully, I'd found my balance, but something in his look now, and the words he'd spoken, told me that patience wasn't today's lesson.

"This last year has been one full of tests, big and small, which have been mastered and passed with relative ease. I fear that the conquering of those battles has caused us to lose sight of the war, and for that, I blame myself."

"Uncle Umar, you carry no blame because..."

He held up his hands to silence my words, and I respectfully put my lips together obediently.

"When I married you and Tynesha, I truly believed that I saw forever in you two, but I could not know the demons that were at work against you. I know that you saw that forever too, which is why you integrated her into your life so completely as to allow her access to all the doors open to you."

The cold chill that suddenly streaked through my body caused my breathing to stutter as I realized that I'd completely forgotten all about making Ty's DNA part of my security protocol. This was a huge oversight on my behalf, and I knew that my uncle wouldn't mention this unless it was a costly one.

"What did she take?" I asked.

"You misunderstand, David. She hadn't taken anything material, but I fear that she is in possession of something valuable."

"What's that?" I asked, fighting against the impatience I felt bubbling up from my soul.

The response to this question came in the form of my uncle reaching into his inner suit jacket pocket and pulling out a sheet of paper that he handed me. I opened it, read it, and then read it again before I let it drop to the table in between us.

"Where did you get this?" I asked shakily.

"I still have friends in the States, but it was more so dumb luck."

"You don't believe in luck, Uncle, only destiny." I reminded him.

The smile that he gave me acknowledged that I was right, but that victory was hollow when compared to the devastating truth that I'd just read.

"I don't understand though. I mean, why expose the truth now? What does she gain, or what is her plan?" I asked, thinking out loud.

"You're assuming that this was her doing though."

"What do you mean?" I asked, confused.

"Follow my train of thought for a moment. Let's say that Tynesha wasn't lying to you, that she was simply lying convincingly enough to Roland in order to stay alive. If that was the case, then she was never really worried about who her child's father was because she knew who it was. She knew that it was you, David."

What he was suggesting made my stomach flip with nauseousness, but it wasn't the first time I'd considered this possibility. Except every time I considered it, my mind went back to the images scorched into my brain of her being fucked by Roland.

"Why send me the video then?"

"I'm afraid that may simply be your demons coming back to haunt you. Honestly, that's the only thing that makes sense," he replied.

The simplicity of his answer only heightened my frustration because it forced me to take blame for the lies he'd warned me not to let catch up to me. He'd told me to tell Ty about Tesha and her mom, but I refused to listen.

"Okay, so by your train of thought, you're saying that these DNA results and the test in general might not have come from Ty? So, that would mean that Roland did it?" I asked.

"Wouldn't you get a DNA test if the baby you were raising as your own suddenly didn't look like you or feel like yours? Assuming that's what happened, it makes sense that he would get a DNA test done."

"I don't know, Unc. That's a hell of a theory, but we need more than a random DNA test to put facts behind these assumptions."

"I agree, and that's why I bought us some time. The results that I gave you were the real results, but because we don't know the situation or the possible danger, I had the results switched to favor Roland. That should give you time to decide how to kill him," he said.

"Good morning, Uncle Umar. Who are we talking about killing?" Shaomi asked, walking toward us.

Chapter 4

(Tynesha) (Texas)

"Hey, little man. You hungry? Is Mama's baby crying because he's hungry?" I asked, picking Rashon up out of his crib.

His wails immediately quieted down to a softer crying, but as soon as he spotted the bottle in my hand, he shut the fuck up. It was comical how his focus was locked on the bottle to the point that he was leaning down and reaching his tiny hand toward it.

"Just wait a minute, fatness," I said, laughing as I carried him from our bedroom out into the living room.

Once I was comfortable on the couch, I cradled him in my arms and popped the bottle in between his waiting lips. The fact that his first drink was so deep and so long that he immediately had to gasp for breath made me laugh again as I pulled the bottle back from him.

"Slow down, Rashon. It's not going anywhere," I said before giving him his meal back.

At three months old, he was definitely fat and healthy, and just as greedy as his nothing ass daddy. Thankfully, he looked more like me than anyone, but every time I looked at him, I saw David, and my heart ached. Of course, I pushed the pain away while praying that Roland would never see in Rashon what I did. God only knew how that would end for me and my son. I'd lived through so many emotions in the last year that I felt like I'd aged ten years in that time span,

24

but the rainbow at the end of every storm was my baby. In the darkest part of my heart, I knew that the solace found in my son was bittersweet at best, but my sanity depended on my ability to focus on the sweet and forget the bitter.

"I love you so much, Rashon," I whispered, planting a kiss on his forehead.

His hazel brown eyes stared at me with love unconditional, and even though he was just a baby, I could swear that he understood me even now. If by some miracle beyond my comprehension he'd been able to hear my thoughts and apologies while I'd been pregnant, then I knew he understood me. All I could do was hope that one day he'd be able to forgive me for the decisions that I'd made. The sound of the front door to the house opening shifted my thoughts, causing me to mentally drop one of the many masks I wore in this version of life I was living.

"Ty? You home?" Roland called out.

"In the living room, bae."

Immediately, I heard the sound of his heavy booted footsteps moving in our direction, and I braced for whatever was to come.

"How's Daddy's little man?" he asked, focusing his attention on Rashon.

I couldn't deny the recognition that had begun to light up my son's eyes whenever Roland was around, and that was just another thing that hurt my soul. My only means of combating the guilt that I felt for robbing David of his right to be a father to Rashon was to remind myself that he had more than enough kids to keep him busy. I knew the pain that he felt in an intimate way, and sometimes, that made me want to hurt his bitch ass even more. The only reason that I hadn't made good on my promise yet was because of Rashon, and for his sake, I didn't want to murder his sisters. At least not today.

"Do you wanna finish feeding him?" I offered.

I wanted a few moments to clear my head and prevent the screaming voices from chorusing.

"Yeah, I got him."

I waited until Roland sat down, and then, I carefully transferred Rashon into his arms without making him relinquish his bottle. I got up off the couch and immediately headed outside into the early evening dusk settling around our quiet suburban neighborhood. For any other woman, this life would probably be a slice of heaven. Roland had gotten us set up in a nice, four-bedroom house on the outskirts of Austin, and he'd found a way to secure our future by getting a job with the local police. I had no idea how many favors he'd had to call in, but I did know that this new life came with some old baggage in the form of him being in bed with the Mexican cartel. I didn't ask questions. I just played my role as a kept woman, and everything was as right as rain from Roland's point of view. He undoubtedly saw shit like everyone from the outside looking in, and that was why he was clueless to my misery. No one had any idea how frequently I daydreamed about locking all the doors and windows in our pretty little house and burning that bitch to the ground with everyone inside. To Roland's credit, he'd ceased treating me like a prisoner ever since I gave him some pussy, but I was still a prisoner of my own making. There was no way out of it for me, and the deeper that realization became, the more hopeless I felt. If this was how postpartum depression felt, then there was no wonder bitches gave the fuck up. I stood on our front porch, simply looking out at the world that was nothing more than an illusion for real, contemplating grabbing the AR-15 out of Roland's police cruiser and redefining the words 'shooting rampage.' I resisted the temptation though, and instead, I walked a slow lap around the block, trying my best to think about absolutely nothing. As I approached our house from the other side, I felt the reluctance in my steps, but I focused on putting my mask back into place before I opened the front door. Once I was back inside, I headed for the kitchen so that I could start making dinner like a good wife, even though the nigga that I'd be cooking for wasn't my husband.

"How the fuck did I get here?" I asked aloud.

"What do you mean?" Roland asked, startling me as he breezed into the room.

"Nothing, I-I just don't know what to make you for dinner, and you know that I'm never at a loss for ideas when it comes to food."

"Don't I know it? Shit, I've gained thirty pounds in the past year, and only increased exercise keeps me from being a fat ass, sloppy nigga," he replied.

"I can stop cooking if you want."

"I wasn't suggesting that, bae, but how about we go out tonight instead? I'll call the babysitter, and then, we can go out for a celebratory meal at Ruth Chris," he offered.

His tone gave away the fact that something had him excited, and that made me look at him with blatant suspicion.

"Celebrate? What are we celebrating, Roland?"

His response was to cross the room until he was standing beside me at the kitchen counter, and then, he put a piece of paper in front of me. As soon as I saw the heading at the top broadcasting that the following were DNA paternity results, I felt my heart stop, and I quit breathing. I didn't reach for the paper because I knew that the shaking of my hand would be too pronounced to hide, so I could only let my eyes move for me. By the time I'd read the results three times over, I felt my head shaking involuntarily.

"I don't-I don't understand," I mumbled.

"What do you mean? It says that Rashon is definitely my son."

The word that sounded off in my mind was LIES, but I fought the urge to scream that out and quickly adjusted my thoughts to avoid my truth from being spoken.

"So, you-you ran a DNA test? You went behind my back, swabbed my muthafuckin son, and ran a DNA test, nigga?" I growled through clenched teeth, turning to face him.

"Yeah, I mean, do you blame me? With all the shit that has happened in the last year and a half, I'd be a sucka nigga not to question any and everything that came out of your mouth."

"Fuck you, you bitch ass nigga!" I said aggressively, slapping him as hard as I could.

The moment that I connected with his face, I realized that I was running on pure adrenaline. Had I not been, I would've hit him with a closed fist because the price I'd pay was the same regardless. Before I could duck, he grabbed me by the throat, slammed me into the nearest wall, and then lifted me off of my feet.

"Bitch, you know better," he growled, squeezing with relentless force.

I could feel the truth of his increased workout regimen, but it was too late for me to panic, and my heart was ten times colder than the last time that we'd fought. Out of reflex, I let my foot fly, and I felt the warmth of his nuts on the tops of my toes through his uniform pants. Instantly, my ability to breathe was restored, and I felt my feet reconnect with the earth, but I was already moving instead of basking in the small victories. As he doubled over and grabbed his prize possessions, to try and stop the pain that he was undoubtedly feeling on his stomach, I was going for the Glock .40 in his holster. I yanked the gun free and put it to his temple.

"Fuck what that paper says, bitch. You'll never be a father to my son... or my daughter," I vowed.

Before he could utter a word, I pulled the trigger, bouncing his head off of the kitchen cabinet as his blood and brain matter stained the beautiful cherry wood. Once his body slumped to the floor, I kicked him over on his back, stood over top of him, and pushed five more bullets into his face to ensure that his spirit felt my hatred. The sight of what would surely be a closed casket funeral didn't make me squeamish or sick in any kind of way. In fact, all I felt was relief, and I found myself taking my first deep breath in longer than I could remember. I took a full thirty seconds to just breathe and memorize what I was seeing before my brain began screaming insistently with one word. Run! With the gun still in my hand, I walked out of the kitchen and went back into my bedroom to check on Rashon. His angelic self was fast asleep in his crib, which would give me the time I needed to get our shit together. None of what had happened was planned, and I wasn't about to waste time trying to pack a bunch of shit, but a smart bitch like me always kept a go-bag. I moved from Rahson's side and went to the closet, moving all of my sneaker boxes out of the way until I could grab my Louis Vuitton roll-carry suitcase. I didn't inspect the contents because I knew that inside was clothes, money, my passport, and three registered handguns. That was enough to start over. I pulled the suitcase up beside the crib, and then, I ran around the room, gathering all of the things I needed to stack my son's diaper bag. By the time I was finished with that, my paranoia was going ape shit because I could have sworn that I was hearing sirens not far from our house. The benefit to living in a gated community was that even cops had to stop before coming into the neighborhood. It wasn't like David's building where they could be denied entry, but I would at least see them at the gates. Just to calm my nerves, I took a quick peek out of the bedroom window, and then, I made my way back to the kitchen. I hurriedly went through Roland's pockets until I found the keys to his office, and then, I made a mad dash toward the farthest bedroom at the back of the house because that was his sanctuary.

I had no idea what lay behind this door, but my gut told me to find out before I burned this bitch to the ground on my way out. After unlocking all three locks guarding the door, I opened it and stepped inside. At first, I didn't understand what I was seeing because there were three different computer monitors showing dozens of camera angles rotating. I immediately recognized our neighborhood and the houses in it, but what drew my attention was the various angles from inside our house. I saw Roland's body in the kitchen from two different angles, but my eyes skated right past that and locked on the four angles by which I could see our bedroom. The cameras were strategically positioned not to show Rashon's crib, but our bed was front and center. The logical reason for this that popped into my mind was that Roland was simply paranoid about me cheating, but then, I looked at the screen a little closer. The tiny red camera icon in the corner of the laptop's screen let me know that this was live footage, and that was when I noticed that every camera boasted the same icon, including the two in the kitchen. I didn't have time to analyze this fully though because, at that exact moment, I saw the Austin police SWAT team come to a skidding halt at the front gate. Instinctively, I grabbed the laptop in front of me and bolted from the room at a dead run to get to Rashon. As I tossed the laptop and the Glock .40 in the suitcase, wrapped the diaper bag around me, and grabbed Rashon, my mind was running in overdrive. There was only one location where there were no cameras, and that was where I headed, moving like my life depended on it because it did.

Chapter 5

(Tesha)

Part of me thought that the decision I'd made to have Royal investigate the family, that I now viewed as opps, would leave me feeling anxious, but I wasn't feeling anything like that. The calm that I'd felt since my conversation with him was foreign to me but welcome because I was so over feeling like a basket case. I didn't know what Royal had planned because we didn't discuss it anymore throughout our day. We just spent time together as a family with Stormy. Despite my misgivings about raising her in virtual isolation, I had to admit that Royal was providing a life for us that I couldn't have dreamed of. As I sat watching him play with Stormy on the bearskin rug in our bedroom, I couldn't help but to smile despite the unimaginable pain that I constantly felt. Moments like this became snapshots of memories that I hung onto, and I was sad that my mom would never meet her granddaughter like this. In a way, I felt responsible for my mother's death. I couldn't help acknowledging that my decision to show her the secret video of David and I fucking that first night had changed everything from that point on. I'd had no doubt that she'd keep my secret, but I hadn't counted on my secret motivating her to become part of the circus including David. As a result, she'd gotten too close to me, to him, and to all the bullshit that Tynesha had set in motion. My mother should be here, and my child should be playing with hers.

"Babe?" Royal whispered.

"Huh?"

The sound of his voice startled me out of my thoughts, and I found him standing right in front of me.

"T, you good?"

"Yeah, I'm-I'm fine. Why?" I asked, looking up and seeing the concern on his face.

"You're crying."

My hand instinctively went to my cheek, and I was shocked to find moisture there because I had no idea when I even started shedding tears.

"Oh, wow, I didn't... I don't know what the fuck happened. I'm okay. I was just thinking about my mom," I explained.

"I understand. Believe me. You know that we can go back and visit her grave whenever you're ready," he replied gently.

With everything that had happened, I'd never got a chance to say goodbye or even see my mom before the ground swallowed her. Royal made sure that she had a proper funeral and a beautiful rose marble headstone on her grave in Georgia. That had only made me love him more.

"One day, I'll go back. One day... What's up though?"

When I glanced past him, I could see Stormy laying on her back, playing contently with the toys suspended above her head that were a part of the blanket she was laying on.

"I just wanted to let you know that I'm gonna go get some work done," he replied.

"Are you gonna be in your office?"

"No, I'm going down to the yacht just in case," he said, staring at me intensely.

I didn't have to ask what 'just in case' meant because I knew that if he found any threats against us then he wasn't going to waste time with his next move. I understood that all of this had to be done, but a huge part of me didn't want him to leave. At least not like this.

"I need something before you go. No questions asked," I said.

His hesitation was brief, but I could see the lights of curiosity shining in his eyes like New York City after dark. When he gave me his nod of acquiescence, I grabbed my phone off of the nightstand, hopped off the bed, and quickly left the room. I found the number that I was looking for immediately, but I waited until I was in the downstairs library with both doors closed before I hit send. It took two rings before my call was answered, and a familiar voice came on the line.

"Is everything okay?"

"Yeah, Free, we're good, but I-uh-I wanted to talk to you about something."

"Okay. It sounds serious, so what's up?" she replied cautiously.

I took a deep breath, and then, I spoke for a straight ten uninterrupted minutes. At the conclusion of my pitch, all I heard was Free breathing for a few moments, and then, she chuckled.

"You're a brave bitch. I'll give you that," she said.

"I've come too far to be scared now."

"I agree, but you need to remember that some bells can't be silenced. This is the mob you're fucking with," she warned.

"I understand that, and the only reason I'm doing it is because I love Royal more than I ever imagined I could love another human being."

My words caused Free to go quiet again, but I felt no apprehension about it at this point because I knew that she loved her brother as fiercely as I did. That was the reason I'd come to her first, even though I knew Royal had great relationships with all of his siblings.

"Okay, Tesha, I got you. And I'll get everyone there in an hour. I'll take care of the details personally to make sure everything goes as smooth as possible."

"Thank you so much, Free, and I promise that you won't regret this," I vowed.

"I know that, sis. We're family."

Before I could respond to her words, the line went dead, and I was left speechless and fighting tears of joy. I never thought that I would have Free's approval, but to have her acceptance was even crazier to me! Now wasn't the time to fall apart emotionally though because that was sure to come. After wiping my face and taking deep breaths to regain my composure, I left the library and headed back to our bedroom. I walked in to find Royal sitting on the loveseat under the window across from the fireplace, gently rubbing Stormy's back as she lay on his chest with her eyes closed. Instinctively, I held my phone up and snapped the picture, and then, I sent it out in a group text between his sisters and me. He looked at me with a raised eyebrow, but all I did was smile and blow him a kiss on my way to my walk-in closet. Given the weather conditions that we faced in Russia, there was hardly ever an excuse to wear any type of dresses, but luckily, there had been events that we'd attended that required formal attire. I grabbed an emerald-green, strapless, Gucci dress that hugged my curves and made my hazel green eyes stand out like a beautiful tiger's. I opted for no shoes though because, as my luck would have it, my toes were the matching shade of green to compliment my dress. After concealing it back inside the black travel bag that I kept it hanging up in inside my closet, I walked out and into Royal's closet, where I grabbed him a black, Tom Ford tux with matching Tom Ford loafers.

"Get dressed," I instructed, laying his clothes on the bed.

I saw the confusion on his face, but before he could put Stormy down to ask me any questions, I'd grabbed my body wash and my bag, and I was back out the door. I ran to the south wing of the castle, knowing that he'd have to search a lot of rooms in between here and there if he came looking for me. Once I picked a room, I hopped in the shower and bathed quickly, and then, I slid the smooth, silk fabric onto my soft, naked skin. The beauty of youth was that I didn't need make-up because my fresh face look could grace the cover of any magazine, but I still hoped Royal would like how I looked, especially when time caught up with me. He was the only man who had ever made me nervous, and it was in the best possible way, even though it was a completely new experience. I loved how he made me feel, and that was a great reason to step into forever. The finishing touches came with me swooping my hair up into a messy bun just as my phone vibrated from an incoming text message. Since Free knew that Royal was in the blind about my request, she'd been smart enough to text me when they entered the compound, so I went to meet them at the front door. By the time I got downstairs and out front, there were two Range Rovers coming to a stop at the bottom of the concrete steps that led up to our front door. I had no doubt that Royal could see all of this from the bedroom room windows if he was looking, and his curiosity was probably killing him. Free, Angel, Destiny, and Madeline climbed out of one SUV, while Bone, Lil Boy, Big Baby, and FatherGod got out of the other one. Seeing this group of powerful, deadly people would make the average person scared enough to need an immediate bathroom break, but the feelings inside me were giddy. They all fell into a line and came up the steps with FatherGod leading the pack, and he stopped right in front of me. His 6'5", three hundred plus pounds cast a huge shadow, which had been terrifying the first time we'd met, but by now, I knew that he wouldn't hurt me.

"Are you really this crazy?" he asked, looking down at me.

"Absolutely," I replied with a straight face.

My response made him laugh, and then, I found myself wrapped up in his massive embrace and being carried back inside the house. Once he put me back on my feet, he turned around to address everyone following us.

"You all help Tesha transform this place, and somebody get with the kitchen staff because we need food and drink to celebrate. I'll go get my son."

The men all headed toward the kitchen, which wasn't any different from them most of the time when they came over, and that left just us women. Before I realized it, and without a word, I found myself surrounded on all sides, but I was surprised to find Angel standing toe to toe with me instead of Free.

"You've grown on us, Tesha, and I admit that it was a pleasant surprise because initially, we were taking over/under bets on your life expectancy. You made us believers in who you said you were though, and I respect that," Angel said.

"Don't feel bad, sweetheart. I got it way worse because they are deadly protective over their dad," Madeline said, smiling.

"We're that way about everyone in our family," Free said.

"And now that includes you," Destiny said from behind me.

"That means we'll kill for you and with you, but there's one thing we won't tolerate. We don't fight each other," Angel stated.

"I know, and I get it," I replied.

"Do you?" Free asked.

"Yes, I do. Royal told me what happened between you all and your mother and then between you and him," I replied honestly.

Angel's eye's flickered toward Free, and then, she looked past me toward Destiny. I could sense the collective surprise that was felt by all the women around me, but I also knew that they understood just how much Royal trusted me if he told me that truth.

"Not one of our finest moments but a lesson that was literally learned through blood, sweat, and tears. We're stronger from that experience," Free said.

"What we need you to know and understand is that you being a part of this family, in the way you've requested, means that you forever forsake all others. It don't matter if they're of blood relations or not. It's our family over everything," Angel stated passionately.

I took my time looking from woman to woman before I turned to give Destiny the same respect.

"In my heart, I made that decision a long time ago, so this is only making it official on paper," I replied genuinely.

"Something that you should know is that we put our own work in around here," Destiny said.

"Meaning what?" I asked.

"Meaning that when the time comes, and it WILL come, for you to prove your loyalty by taking a life to save ours and our way of life, that you won't hesitate. You'll drop the hammer on whoever poses a threat," Free explained.

"On the soul of my daughter, I swear that I will," I vowed without hesitation.

Angel nodded in apparent approval, and then, she pulled a dark blue ring box from her pocket.

"You're gonna need this then," she said, passing the box to me.

I opened it and what I saw made me gasp immediately.

"Oh, my God, it's gorgeous!" I exclaimed, completely mesmerized by the sheer size of the diamond protruding from the box.

"Seven carat flawless diamond solitaire with a platinum reenforced band covered with another three carats worth of diamonds," Madeline said with appreciation in her voice.

"This is a blood diamond, but not in the traditional sense. Someone died for you to be able to wear that, and I was the one who took their life. I'm giving it to you because it's symbolic in multiple ways, and because I was the first one of us that Royal trusted, so our bond is different. I'm trusting you with him and his heart, and if you fuck up, then you'll pay in blood until there's nothing left of you," Angel promised.

"I understand, and I'm honored," I said sincerely.

"Olay then. Let's get you two married," Madeline said, taking me by the hand.

Chapter 6

(Royal)

My mind was on fire with the flames of curiosity blazing in every corner because, for the life of me, I couldn't figure out what Tesha was up to. I was hesitant to get dressed up, but when I saw the family pull up, I knew that there had to be a good reason for them to be here. Knowing Tesha, it was probably a family dinner because she loved those. And if she had something she only wanted to say once, then that was where she did it. I still didn't know why I had to get dressed up, but her happiness was worth the inconvenience.

"I see that you finally learned how to tie that bow tie without me."

"You taught me well, Pops," I replied, turning away from inspecting myself in the bedroom mirror to find him standing in the doorway.

"I guess I did... but I'm wondering now if you've learned the most important lesson that I ever tried to teach you."

Out of reflex, I started to ask him what he meant, but I paused for a moment to contemplate, and then, I smiled.

"That nothing in this world is more important than family, not even money or power," I replied confidently.

The smile that he gave me was as familiar as the fingers on my hand because I saw it every time I looked in the mirror.

"It's good to know that you've paid attention because you're about to embark on the next part of this journey called family, and it's only gonna get harder."

"What do you mean?" I asked.

"Being a part of a family is different from having your own family. When you get your own family, you become the head of that family, and sometimes, in order to protect them, you have to become the head of that monster. You understand?"

"Yeah, I get it now. The last year has taught me a lot, but shit got beyond real once Stormy was born. Having a child, and being responsible for that child, is something that can only be grasped through experience. I thought that I knew everything that I needed to know through experience when I had my brother and my nephew with me on the run, but I didn't. I see now that I could've fucked their lives up, and in some ways, I did," I admitted.

"Maybe, but that's not today's problem. Today, you take the next step as a man, a father, a gangster, and a husband," he said, tossing a ring box at me.

Luckily for good reflexes that I caught it out of midair because I didn't take my eyes off of my father.

"A h-husband?"

"I can tell that your surprise is genuine, and that probably makes me love Tesha more. Just open the box and don't panic," he said, chuckling.

I did as he instructed, and what I found caused my heart to gallop.

"I-I've seen this ring before, Dad."

"I'm only a little surprised by that considering that it was the ring that your mom gave me after Destiny was born," he replied.

I glanced up to see a nostalgic look on his face, and I knew that this was a rare moment because he never talked about, or showed any emotion about, my mother. I had never pressed the issue because his memories, like his pain, were his own.

"I saw a picture of you and her where your arms were wrapped around her, and this ring was visible. I remember asking her why there were so many stones inside the platinum band."

"A blue sapphire, a red ruby, a green emerald, and a flawless diamond. They symbolized your mom and your sisters because all of our children were priceless jewels," he said softly.

I nodded while looking back down at the ring in the box, trying to suppress my overwhelming desire to shed a tear. Just based on the tone of his voice, I knew how much this ring meant to my parents, and I made a silent vow to represent it the right way.

"A husband, huh? Well, it feels like a good day to get married," I said, smiling widely.

"I'm glad that you think so because I doubt if your bride to be would take no for an answer at this point."

We both laughed, and I knew that my pops was right, but Tesha being who she was only made me love her more for real.

"I don't have a ring for her," I said, suddenly realizing this fact.

"Don't worry about that. Your sisters are with Tesha, and they came prepared, which means that all you have to do is show up. Now, where's my granddaughter?"

"Asleep in her crib over there," I said, pointing.

"Alright, well, I've got her, and you go downstairs to the kitchen to make sure we've got enough food and drink for a party. You know how we do."

"Alright, Pops," I said, crossing the room to give him a hug, and then, I turned to leave.

When I got to the kitchen, Bone was talking to the personal chef that I'd hired because I'd wanted Tesha to eat as healthy as possible while she'd been pregnant. Lil Boy and Big Baby were sitting on one of the kitchen counters, eating out of a big bag of chips and laughing at something.

"What's so funny?" I asked, walking up.

"Listening to Bone trying to explain in Russian that we want soul food for your wedding. Bruh is straight up butchering these peoples' language," Lil Boy replied, shaking his head.

I laughed out loud as I looked back over to where Bone and the chef were standing.

"Y'all ain't shit! Why you let him do the talking?" I asked.

Big Baby immediately pointed toward his mouth and gave me a smirk, which caused Lil Boy to start laughing again.

"Nah, my nigga, you can quit playing like you still can't or won't talk because I know that's cap. I heard you and Destiny fucking one day, and I KNOW that it wasn't her voice sounding like James Earl Jones," I said, laughing.

Suddenly, Big Baby started choking on the chips that he'd been shoveling in between his lips, causing Lil Boy to hammer him on the back while we both laughed hysterically at him. Lil Boy and Big Baby were brothers, raised together and everything, so Lil Boy had vouched for the fact that Big Baby didn't talk. We'd all taken that to mean that he couldn't talk, but apparently, that sister of mine knew sorcery because I knew damn well that I'd heard him speak before - even if it did sound like it was in tongues.

"What the hell are you fools over here doing?" Bone asked, joining us at the kitchen counter.

"The usual," I replied.

"Which means bullshitting," Bone said, nodding and smiling.

Bone was Free's husband and her right hand of God, but he'd grown up in the streets of Atlanta with Lil Boy and Big Baby too. They were all thicker than thieves, and outside of my dad, they were the only men I'd looked up to in my life.

It was good to have them here now because with Lil Boy married to Angel and Big Baby married to Destiny, I knew that these men had wisdom to pass down.

"Is this shit crazy? I mean, are we too young for this?" I asked seriously.

"You ask that question like you're still a kid or something. When was the last time you were allowed to be a child, or even desired a child's life?" Bone asked.

"Yeah, you're right, but marriage is a real grown man game," I replied.

"True, and that's why having the right partner makes all the difference in the world," Lil Boy said.

"I won't go so far as to say that Tesha is cut from the same cloth as your sisters, but in time, I think that she will be. She's good people," Bone stated.

"Plus, she ain't no scary ass female, considering that she stepped into a room with all of us as soon as you all got to Russia," Lil Boy pointed out.

I was only an inch shorter than my pops, but that nigga had bigger muscles than me. Big Baby was a stocky muthafucka that looked like he could run through a tank, and Bone carried his weight the same way. Lil Boy was damn near seven feet tall though, so his size was the most imposing, but baby had still stepped into the pack of wolves without fear or hesitation. It was the beginning of her earning the family's trust and respect, and it was what led to this moment.

"I can't lie. I've known from the jump that Tesha was different than anything I'd run across. I didn't just want to fuck with her; I wanted to build with her. You know?" I asked, looking around at the men before me.

Every man nodded while smiling.

"You're ready, Royal, and don't worry because it only hurts for a second," Bone said.

"What only hurts for a second?" I asked, confused.

"That tight ass bow tie," Lil Boy said, swiftly reaching up and pulling it undone.

We all laughed, and then, Bone stepped in front of me to retie it. By the time he finished, Free was coming into the kitchen toward us.

"It's time," she said, reaching for my hand.

After two deep breaths, I took ahold of her hand and followed her lead. My steps were sure, and the butterflies that I could feel in my stomach were the good kind, so I knew that I wasn't afraid. When Free opened the doors to the library, I was shocked to see candles and an aisle that was made out of different color rose petals leading to the middle of the room. Angel and Destiny stood on one side, and Madeline stood in the middle.

"Where's Dad?" I asked once we got to the makeshift altar where Madeline stood, ready to perform the ceremony.

Free let my hand go and stood opposite Angel and Destiny, but no one spoke a word to answer my question. Suddenly, the lights dimmed, allowing the beauty of the candlelight to reign supreme. I felt a physical jolt of emotion rip through my body, and at that moment, I knew that Tesha had entered the room. When I turned to look behind me, I saw my pops standing there with Stormy in one arm and Tesha's arm looped through his other arm. I could feel my smile spreading with ease and love as I silently watched them move toward me. When my pops stopped in front of me, he handed Stormy to me while looking me in the eyes.

"You're the head of this family, son. Remember that."

"I will," I vowed, accepting my daughter with open arms.

We turned to face Madeline, and Tesha moved up beside me. The exchanging of vows took about ten minutes, but we poured our hearts out to each other. By the time we were done, everyone, including us, was in tears. The kiss to seal our union was the sweetest thing I'd ever known, and for the first time in my life, I could honestly say that my heart was completely full. After the ceremony, I danced with my new bride to a song by Teddy Swims called *Lose Control*, and I was singing the lyrics softly in her ear, which made her cry all over again. From that point on, we partied. Good food, good music, and family was all that we knew until the early morning hours.

As part of our wedding present, my sisters kidnapped Stormy so that we could be alone for the night, and once the doors closed behind them, we wasted no time appreciating the solitude. We made love for hours, refusing to let each other reach that ultimate climax, and instead, we battled for supremacy. We explored different rooms in the castle, which only heightened the thrill because we were christening virgin territory and creating lasting memories. Finally, we came together, with her on top, pinning my back to the mattress in our bedroom with her hands on my chest. I didn't feel like I'd lost in the slightest though because she came so hard that she literally passed out from orgasmic bliss right on my chest. I laid there, holding her and listening to the cute sound of her occasional snores. I had no doubts that this was the one and only woman that I was supposed to be with, and I felt so grateful to have her. I could only hope that my mother was looking down and accepting this woman for her only son.

I laid in bed with Tesha for at least a half an hour before I carefully and gently moved her off of me and over on to her side of the bed. After that, I eased out of our bed and silently slipped into my closet where I threw on some clothes, and then, I made my way to my office a few doors down from our bedroom. Once I was inside, I brought my computer online so that I could check on some things, but I was hit by an immediate surprise in the form of my wife's face being on an FBI wanted poster. It took me a full ten seconds to quiet the panic and realize that it wasn't Tesha they were looking for; it was Tynesha, and the charges were worthy of a death sentence. That spelled disaster for her, but it could be fortuitous for me and my family if I played it right. I had to move fast, which meant that I would have to work while I was on the move. I made a quick call to the staff aboard my yacht, telling them to expect me within the hour and be ready to set sail. I knew what it would mean if I woke Tesha up, so I decided to write a note instead so that she would have some understanding at least. It didn't feel right to leave, regardless of whether or not she would be understanding, because I really just didn't want to be away from her. It was like my pops had told me though; this was my family, and that meant that their safety was my responsibility. It was time for me to be that monster.

Chapter 7

(David)

The panic I felt at seeing Shaomi made me want to snatch the paper off the table and shred it fast, but instead, I pushed it back toward my uncle. I did this while standing up and pulling a chair out for Shaomi, making sure to smile naturally and kiss her on the cheek.

"Are you hungry, sweetheart?" I asked.

"Yep, and I already told the cook what to bring us all. So, catch me up and tell me who you're gonna kill and why," she said.

When I turned back around, I noticed no sign of the DNA results, which slightly relieved me but not by much because I knew that Shaomi was like a grave digger when it came to being nosy.

"We were just discussing killing Roland," Umar replied.

"Well, it's about damn time. Do you know where Roland and Ty are hiding?" she asked.

"Last time I checked, they weren't exactly hiding. It just wasn't any way in to get to them without the world collapsing on our head. I give credit where credit is due, and Roland is a worthy adversary because he was able to rise from the ashes of his fractured relationship with Zoe Pound to build an alliance with the Mexican cartel. He definitely doesn't mind sharing a bed with insane and ruthless bedfellows," Umar stated.

"Anyone can get got though, so what's the plan?" Shaomi asked eagerly.

"We ain't got that far yet, but whatever it is won't involve you," I said firmly.

"What? Why not? Bae, you know that I got your back, and I can…"

"You can sit your pretty ass in this nice mansion and raise our children," I said.

"Excuse me?" she replied, looking at me like I'd lost my damn mind.

"What my nephew is trying to say, Shaomi, is that you just gave birth to a happy, healthy baby boy who needs you."

"He needs his daddy too, but that's not gonna keep David here, is it? My question is why now though? Did something happen?" she asked.

"Something like what?" I asked.

"I don't know... Maybe you found out that Ty's baby is yours, and now this is a rescue mission," she replied, glaring at me.

Time stopped instantly as my mind scrambled to find the words that would lessen the blow that was the truth, but I never got the chance to use them.

"Actually, the baby isn't David's, and I literally started the conversation off telling him the very same thing," Umar said smoothly.

The look on Shaomi's face was clearly skeptical, but I was just a spectator at this point, so I was looking at my uncle too. He calmly pulled his phone out and began searching for something. Once he found it, he slid his phone to her, and she read the results out loud off of the screen before turning to look at me.

"So, you wanna kill him because he got your bitch pregnant? Is that it?" she asked with apparent disdain.

"No, I'mma kill him because he needs killing," I replied calmly.

"What about Ty? You know that she needs to die too," she insisted.

"On that I think we all agree," Umar replied, nodding his head.

"I don't see any scenario where she lives, and I ain't looking for one," I stated.

I could still see skepticism on her face, but she wisely held her tongue.

"Daddy, Prince David threw up!" Dayjah yelled from the balcony door.

"Okay, baby. He's okay. It's natural," I replied, looking at her.

She nodded once and disappeared back inside the house.

"I'll go check on him real quick because, if not, she'll worry herself into a tantrum," Shaomi said, shaking her head as she stood up.

"It is good that she is so protective of her little brother already because most kids would be jealous of all the attention they're not getting. Your kids will be close," Umar predicted.

"They damn well better be because they only have each other. Well, until we have more kids," she said, smiling at me as she walked away.

Neither my uncle nor I spoke until the veranda contained just us, but my mind was working with a machine's precision.

"It's a risk for me to go back to the states," I said.

"And yet I know that I couldn't keep you here unless I had you chained up somewhere."

"So, what are you saying?" I asked.

"I'm saying that I understand, and I support your decision to go, David, but I need to know what you're gonna do with the information I gave you."

I sat in silence for a moment because I knew that this situation was too complicated for easy answers to apply. A lot had been done that couldn't be undone, and all of it was worth killing for, but my mission couldn't be to murder everyone. That could cost my son his life.

"Do you know his name? My son?" I asked softly.

"Rashon Porter."

I nodded while absorbing this piece of knowledge and letting it tumble around my brain with the millions of questions that still remained.

"I'm his father, so I'mma do the same thing that I would do for any of my children, and that's keep him safe. This is gonna require finesse though and resources. I know that because of what happened last year, a lot of your friends turned on you, and you lost your diplomatic immunity status as well, so any help you offer can only be from a distance," I said.

"One thing that you must learn, nephew, is that the currency of secrets increases in value with each passing day. I may not have my full diplomatic immunity restored yet, but no doors are still closed to me, and those who turned on me lost their ability to draw breath. This game is ruthless, spelled with all capital letters and no spaces. I play it that way, and no matter how much finesse you use, you must always remember to play it that way as well."

I heard the message that he was sending loud and clear. I just didn't know how to apply it yet.

"What do I do about Shaomi? Do I tell her the truth?" I asked.

"That's a question only you can answer, but I pose another one for you to consider. Is a lie a lie if only you know the truth?"

Instinctively, I started to say yeah, but the longer I thought about that question, the muddier the water got. Right now, the only people who knew that Rashon was my son were me, my uncle, and whoever had run the DNA test that yielded the true results. All I had to do was look at my Uncle Umar to know that he was going to die with the lie, and silencing the lab tech would be easy if it became necessary. This wasn't the time though, which meant I could focus solely on rescuing my son and deal with the fallout of the truth later.

"How soon can you get me back to the states?" I asked.

"As soon as you say the word, the plane will be ready."

"Do it. Texas is a big state, but now that I know my son's name, I can narrow the location because she's had to have taken him to a doctor by now," I rationalized.

"How much support do you need?"

"I got that covered. I've got a few friends that will allow for the finesse that's necessary, but I'll need weapons once I get there," I replied.

"Not a problem. Roland is backed by the Zeta Cartel, so in order to level the playing field, I agreed to supply the Sinola Cartel with a metric ton of fentanyl on consignment. They're definitely our friends now."

Hearing this made me smile, but it was not because of what he'd done. It was the foresight that he had that I loved so much.

"You knew that I would choose war over peace, didn't you?" I asked.

"Of course. You are your father's son, and a better warrior I did not know."

"While we're on the subject of kids and parents, I wanted to ask you if any progress had been made on the other front?" I asked.

His suddenly somber look said the words, but I still waited for him to speak.

"Tesha has still not responded to any messages about you seeing your daughter since the last time she said no. She is protected by Royal and his family, and no one that I know is willing to go up against the Walkers, especially with the rumor that FatherGod is still alive. When he was believed to be dead, people thought that his family would collapse, and when they went to war with each other, people could smell the end of an era. Somehow, it didn't go down like they thought though, and now, they've sufficiently regrouped in

Russia to become an even more dominant force to be feared. It's crazy to go at them anywhere, but taking a run at them in Russia is suicide," he replied.

I'd been doing my best to avoid an all-out war with Royal and his family, but every day that that nigga played daddy to my daughter fucked with my sanity, and I couldn't have that. I'd told Tesha what family meant to me, so for her to keep my child from me was beyond hurtful. It was betrayal.

"We'll figure out how to best move with that situation after I've resolved the other problem, but I'm telling you now that I don't give a fuck WHO those people are. They ain't keeping my kid from me."

"I understand," he replied.

Movement to my right caused me to look toward the veranda door, and I saw Shaomi coming toward us holding Prince David in one arm while Dayjah's hand was wrapped up in her other hand. Following behind them were servants with plates of food in their hands. I pulled the chair out next to me, and Dayjah immediately raced to it.

"Daddy, I got pancakes. Do you want some?"

"No, thank you, baby," I replied, smiling down at her.

"Do you think Prince David can have some, Daddy, because milk isn't enough to fill him up?"

"He's not big enough to eat what you eat, baby, but give it time," I said, accepting her plate with pancakes and eggs from the servant and putting it in front or her.

My own plate contained waffles covered in strawberries, topped with whipped cream, and a side of sausage, but I had too much on my mind to eat. My uncle had the same thing as me, but unlike me, he wasted no time digging into his food.

"Go ahead and eat, bae, and give me Prince," I said, holding my arms out.

"You're not gonna eat?" Shaomi asked, passing him to me.

"I'll eat before I leave," I replied, averting my gaze from hers because I knew the heat was coming.

When I glanced across the table at my uncle, I could tell by his expression that he felt the temperature shift that was imminent, but we both understood that it was unstoppable.

"Leaving? How soon were you planning on leaving?" Shaomi asked calmly.

"Right away because I don't wanna be gone long," I replied, keeping my voice neutral.

Arguing in front of the kids was not something that we did because we vowed to always present a united front, but I didn't know if Shaomi could keep her cool right now.

"Why don't you two go in the house and talk? I'll take Prince David," Umar said, holding his arms out.

As much as I wasn't looking forward to the fight, I knew that the conversation was inevitable, so I got ready to hand my son off, but Shaomi surprised me.

"Uncle Umar, we're good, and I completely understand that this situation needs to be taken care of as soon as possible. Will you be travelling with him?"

"No, there's no room for an old dog to run with these dangerous wolves, so I suspect that I will just putter around the mansion and spend time with the kids," he replied.

"We'll be happy to have you," she said, smiling genuinely.

For a moment, all I could do was look back and forth between Shaomi and my uncle because this was not at all how I expected shit to play out. My instincts were screaming at me that something was way off, but I'd be damned if I opened my mouth and spoke that shit into existence. Instead, I turned my attention on my baby boy, and I covered his face with kisses until he was giggling uncontrollably.

"Don't get too big on me, son," I said, loving how much his smile looked like his mother.

"He won't, Daddy, because you won't let me feed him," Dayjah said with a mouthful of pancakes.

We all laughed at that, which was just what we needed and the beauty of having kids around. No matter what I accomplished in this world, I knew in my heart that being a good dad would be what I was most proud of.

"Don't worry, Dayjah, you can feed Mommy and help me cook too," Shaomi said.

"Lord knows that you love to do both of those things," I said, laughing.

"Well, I've got a good reason to," she replied defensively.

I could see her slide something next to my plate out of my peripheral vision, causing me to turn my attention away from my son. What I saw almost made me drop him on his head accidentally.

"Yoooo," I said, looking over at her.

"You thought it was funny when you popped my stitches, but you must have forgotten how fertile I am, Big Daddy. So, say hello to baby number three in the oven because I'm definitely pregnant."

Chapter 8

(Tynesha)

As soon as my feet touched the grass in the backyard to our house, I sprinted as best I could toward the back gate. I was holding Rashon tightly in one arm while I fumbled with Roland's keys awkwardly in my hand. There was a shed right next to the door in the wooden fence, which was where Roland kept the cartel's dope stashed. That was why there were no cameras in the backyard. I knew that the shed had its own top of the line security system, but that wasn't my destination. By the time I got to the door in the fence, Rashon was wide awake, and pissed off enough to cry about it, which someone was sure to hear if I didn't hurry.

It felt like it took an eternity before the locks were opened, and I was allowed to step through. After quickly shutting the door behind us, I crossed the small patch of dirt that led to the actual gate surrounding the community that I was no longer a part of. Even though my soul was screaming at me to hurry the fuck up, I began to look for the trap door in a slow, methodical way. Based on what Roland had told me, I knew that there had to be a section of this gate where the bars were cut through in order to allow unseen access to the mules who came whenever. At the time that he'd told me this, I'd appreciated the discretion because it meant that he was at least trying to keep business separate from our personal life, but now, I was glad to be able to escape. The sounds of the sirens were drowning out the sounds of

Rashon's screams, but it still tore at my heart to see my little man so upset.

"Hang on, baby. It'll be okay. Just hang on," I said, trying to soothe him.

I put all of my concentration on the gate, and I finally found the section that I was looking for. Without hesitation, I kicked the loose section out, and then, I carefully crouched through with Rashon before pulling the suitcase behind me. From there, I moved with purpose down the short embankment, and then, I crossed the street to the shopping center in the distance. Every fiber of my being wanted to run right now, but in my mind's eye, I could see just how much that behavior would stand out in this sleepy, suburban area. So, I walked at a normal pace, resisting the powerful urge to look backwards over my shoulder by directing my focus on soothing my son. When I stopped running and jostling him around, he stopped screaming, and now, he was just clinging to me while giving the occasional whine to make his displeasure known.

"It's okay, baby boy. Mama's got you. You're okay," I said softly, keeping my eyes on the stores in front of me. No one was paying attention to our approach, which meant that hopefully no one would remember us when we disappeared. The immediate problem was that I had no idea how to pull off this magical Houdini act, and I knew in my soul that I was on borrowed time as far as moving undetected. The first thing that popped into my mind was a carjacking in the fading daylight, even though that would only add to my long list of problems. Before I convinced myself to pull one of the guns out of my suitcase, I spotted an eighteen-wheeler tractor trailer idling on the service road next to the gas station to my left. Immediately, I changed course and headed for the truck, mentally going over what I could say to the driver to help me and my son. The only plan that I could formulate was that nothing was off limits, even if that meant I had to give a nigga some pussy to get us far the fuck away. Just as

I was approaching the back bumper of the trailer, a cute, Black chick rounded the far side of the truck, and our eyes locked. She stopped in her tracks, but I kept moving toward her.

"You okay, Miss?" she asked.

"N-No, he beat me. I need to get out of here," I replied, using just the right pitch to sell the victim role.

Her brown eyes flickered past me before coming quickly back to my face and then down toward Rashon. For a full five seconds, I held my breath and just silently prayed.

"Hop in and go straight to the back of the cab," she instructed, heading for the driver's side door.

I wasted no time rushing around the side of the truck and climbing up into the cab, thanking God the whole way. By the time I got me and Rashon inside with our luggage, she was in the driver's seat, and we slowly pulled off. It took about ten minutes before I could breathe anything like a sigh of relief, and even then, I did it with a lot of caution.

"Th-Thank you so much," I said, wiping silent tears from my face.

"You're more than welcome, sweetheart. Just make sure that you're not doing all of this for nothing."

"What do you mean?" I asked.

"You just took a huge step that most women are afraid to take, and some never get to take it before they lose their lives. Don't let it be for nothing by going back into whatever you're running from. You and your son deserve better."

The wisdom of her words was undeniable, just like the experience that I could hear lacing the words that she spoke. Only I knew that there was no going back to what I was running away from, but I understood why her advice was relevant regardless. Roland had beat me for years, and I'd made excuses for it. Learning from this moment, and from my past, would be the only way to ensure that I didn't end up in this same situation again. Next time, it could be me dead, and then, I would've failed at my responsibility as a mother. My mother had failed me, and I'd be damned if I did mine the same way.

"What's your name?" I asked.

"Vanessa, but you can call me Nessa."

"I wanna thank you again, Nessa, and you can call me Ty. Listen, I've got money if you can just take us..."

"Let me stop you right there, Queen. I don't want your money, and I'll take you and your son anywhere that's on my route. Technically, we're not supposed to have anyone in the rig who doesn't work for the company, but this is something that my boss will understand. She won't understand me veering off course and this shipment being any kind of late," Nessa explained.

"I understand, and I'm not trying to cause you any trouble. Can you tell me which direction you're headed in?"

"I've gotta drop this load in Nogales and then hitch another load that goes southeast into Florida," she replied.

Suddenly, the idea of going back to Florida spoke to me in a way that was comforting, but it only took a few seconds of consideration to realize that it was a false sense of comfort. I'd spent my whole life in Florida, and I had roots there, but after everything that both Roland and David had done, I knew there were too many memories and enemies in that state. I was reasonably sure that I would be safe with Rashon if I headed north to New York with Nyaisha and my family out that way because it was easy to get lost in New York City. The reality that I was now a cop killer though had me more than a little hesitant to paint that type of target on my family by getting them involved. I felt my stomach drop as the reality set in that me and my son were all alone in this world, and it was my fault. More tears clouded my vision before sliding down my face and landing on my precious son's chest. I'd never felt more like a failure in my entire life, but I knew there was no time for self pity parties, no matter how bad I felt. Rashon was depending on me.

"If you drop me off in Nogales, I can walk across into Mexico," I stated, wiping my eyes with the back of my hand.

"Cross into Mexico? With a newborn? I don't mean to tell you what to do or to sound like your mother, but beautiful American women are an endangered species in Mexico."

"Yeah, I know, but I don't have an option," I replied.

She turned and glanced at me for a second before putting her eyes back on the open road.

"I know that you said that you have money on you, but anything else of value you need to hide or get rid of. Starting with that Louis Vuitton bag," she advised.

Her mentioning my luggage made me look down, and I immediately saw the bigger problem.

"Oh, shit!"

"I get it, and I'm sure that it cost a pretty penny, but they'll kill you for it without thinking twice," she said seriously.

"No, it's-it's not that. I've got guns on me. How the fuck am I gonna get across the border with a gun?"

In response to my question, she began pushing buttons, engaging the autonomous driving system, and then, she moved to the back of the cab with us.

"Okay, look, I need you to level with me and tell me if all of this is just as bad as it looks and sounds?" she asked, sitting beside me on the bunk.

"It's worse, but I-I didn't have a choice because..."

She held up her hand to silence me, but she was nodding in understanding.

"How old are you, Ty?"

"I'm twenty-three," I replied.

"That makes me old enough to be your mama, so I'mma give you some free game. If you did what you had to do beyond the shadow of a doubt, then don't carry that regret because that's nothing more than a distraction. Your sole focus right now has to be your survival because it's not just your life that hangs in the balance."

Her words came with a pointed look down at Rashon, but my mind was hundreds of miles away on a decision that I would always regret in part.

"I hear you, and honestly, I've survived worse," I said truthfully.

"Okay, then. I've got a crazy way for shit to work out, but you're gonna have to play your part."

"I can do it, whatever it is," I replied confidently.

"That's easy to say, but the part you play is involving money. Serious money. Do you have that?"

Serious money sounded like more than the $20K I had hidden amongst my clothes in the suitcase, and I felt the beginnings of panic start to work its way through my chest.

"I've got $20K to my name," I admitted.

"That's more than enough to get you into Mexico, but I know that's not your final destination, so what are you gonna do next?"

"I don't know... I just know that I need to get out of this country and keep moving until I'm beyond their reach," I said, hearing the desperation in my own voice.

She stared at me for a long moment, and then, she pulled the phone out of the pocket of her jean jacket. For a split second, the panic that I'd felt rising hit a fever pitch because I didn't know who she was calling, but ultimately, I knew that I was willing to kill her if she betrayed me. For a few moments, all that could be heard was the growl of the truck's engine, and then, Nessa started talking. From what I was able to gather, she was coordinating with her boss to do a quick off the books run into Mexico. Her decisive nod let me know that she got approval, and then, she disconnected the call.

"Okay, so this is the plan. When we get to Nogales, I'm gonna drop this load and pick up one that's not on the manifest. It's dope, cartel dope, and you're gonna pay the $10,000 to the border patrol who's gonna let us cross without checking anything. You won't even have to scan your passport because we were never there. Understand?" she asked.

I nodded and then unzipped the suitcase to dig the money out.

"You still need to get rid of that bag though," she advised.

When I looked up, she was taking stuff out of a plain, black backpack, and then, she passed it to me.

"Can you hold him for a sec?" I asked, handing her the money first.

When she opened her arms to Rashon, I gently handed him off, and then, I quickly transferred all of my worldly possessions into the backpack. I stuffed the remaining $10k down into my panties that I had on, and I tucked my Glock .42 with the laser beam on it into my jeans.

"That's smart," she said, handing me my son back.

"Now what?"

"Well, we've got a couple hours until we reach our destination, so it's probably a good idea for you to get some rest. Who knows when you'll have the chance again?" she replied.

I nodded, and she got off of the bunk so that she could get back into the driver's seat. I laid Rashon down close to the back wall of the cab so that when I laid down beside him, he was barricaded in safely. I doubted that I would be able to sleep, but within half an hour, the gentle vibrations from the truck lulled him straight into dreamland. I laid there watching him sleep while fighting the demons in my mind that kept reminding me of the fault that I carried in all of this. I knew that I wasn't the only one at fault though, and all it took was that thought to cross my mind in order to switch the direction of my racing ideas. Despite the shit that David had done, I didn't spend time focusing my hatred at him because he was nothing more than a nigga following his dick. What he'd done was fucked up but what Tesha and Shaomi had done was what HAD to be answered for. The more that I fixated on that thought, the clearer I started to see my circumstances for what they were. By the time we arrived at the Mexican border, the sun was up, and the storm clouds had parted in my mind. I could now clearly see the rainbow in my future, and to get to it, I just needed to make it rain blood.

Chapter 9

(Tesha)

My sleep had been so peaceful that I had to stretch like an overgrown tabby cat before opening my eyes or attempting to leave our bed.

"Damn, bitch, did you really just wake up with a huge ass grin on your face?"

Even though I immediately recognized Free's voice, I was still startled enough to hop out of my fucking skin and give a slight scream.

"What the fuck, Free?!" I exclaimed, putting my hand to my chest to hold the comforter up over my nakedness.

"Good morning, sunshine. I'd ask you how you're feeling, but your hair explains it all."

"You know what? Fuck you, Free. What are you doing sitting in my room, watching me sleep?" I asked, looking around for my husband.

When my eyes finally landed back on Free, I could tell that she'd gone instantly serious, but she said nothing and instead offered me a piece of paper. I hesitated to accept it, but as soon as I spotted Royal's handwriting, I snatched it from in between her fingertips. There wasn't a lot to read because all he'd said was that he loved me and Stormy, and he'd be home as soon as he was done.

"As soon as he's done what?" I asked, looking up at Free.

"Is that a question you really want an answer to, Tesha?"

"I asked it, didn't I?" I replied, dropping the blanket and swinging my feet to the floor.

"Get dressed and meet us in Royal's office."

I opened my mouth to ask who 'us' was, but she was already headed for the door. I got up with the intention of throwing something on real quick, but the lady in me knew that I smelled like a satisfied whore after what me and my husband had done to each other. So, I hopped in the shower for a quick thorough wash, threw on some jeans with a T-shirt, and then, I went to Royal's office. When I walked through the door, I saw Destiny sitting behind Royal's computer while Free and Angel occupied the brown, leather loveseat beside the fireplace.

"Royal doesn't like anyone to fuck with his computer," I said, feeling suddenly territorial.

"Yeah, I know. I taught him well. Don't worry. He knows that I'm here because this is where he wants me," Destiny replied, not bothering to look away from the screen.

"Okay, well, somebody tell me what the fuck is going on, and where is my daughter?" I asked with rising irritation.

No one responded, but Free got up and came over to me.

"Calm down, sis. We'll tell you everything that you wanna know, but first, you have to truly be sure that you wanna hear it," Free stated in a soft tone.

I resisted the urge to respond with some sarcastic, hot shit, and instead, I took a calming breath to give myself a moment to process what was being asked of me. My mindset was stuck on reacting instead of responding, and I needed to switch gears real quick in order to accomplish clear thinking.

"I wanna know what's going on," I insisted calmly.

Free studied me for a few seconds, and then, she looked at Destiny.

"Come here," Destiny demanded.

I walked to her and stood just over her left shoulder so that I could see the screen.

"What the fuck?" I mumbled, leaning forward to get a better look at the wanted poster that had my face on it.

For a split second, I thought that this was some old shit to do with the governor's son that I was accused of killing, even though I'd gotten that sorted out a while ago. Since it obviously wasn't me, that meant it was my twin, and I quickly read all of the information on the screen.

"Did they release the video to the public?" I asked.

"Part of it but I hacked into the Austin Police Department's database so that I could see everything they had," Destiny replied.

"How did they get it at all? This shit looks like it happened inside their house, and I find it hard to believe that Ty would have cameras in her house," I said, thinking logically.

"There were definitely cameras inside their house, and based on the shit I've found that Roland posted on the dark web, I'd say it's a safe bet that Ty had no idea he was filming their lives," Destiny said.

I felt my stomach roll in disgust, but I pushed it down and refocused my mind on the problem at hand.

"Show me everything connected to Roland's death," I demanded.

As her fingers flew across the keyboard at lightning speed, I looked over at Free and Angel, trying to gauge their thoughts, but they both wore neutral expressions.

"Here we go," Destiny said.

My attention shifted back to the computer screen, and the moment I saw my sister, I felt a hand squeeze my heart for a brief instant. My eyes stayed riveted on the screen as shit went from a seemingly normal day in suburbia to all out mayhem within minutes.

"Play it again," I insisted once the footage of her fleeing the scene with her son ended.

I watched it all over again in silence, committing it to memory, but cautioning myself against feeling anything that resembled pity for the woman on the screen. We were sisters by blood, but we were virtual strangers now, which meant that she wasn't entitled to my pity.

"What the hell did he show her on that paper, and where did she disappear to?" I asked.

"I can't make out what's on the paper, but whatever it was sent her to the next level with rocket fuel in her veins. As for where she disappeared to, that's a question that the cops are still asking. She escaped out of the back of the house because there were no cameras in the backyard. No doubt that was due to the large quantities of heroin and fentanyl they found in a shed back there on their property. From there, she escaped the net they tried to drop on her," Free replied.

"Why do I get the feeling that you know where she's at?" I asked, looking from Destiny, to Angel, to Free.

"Because by now you know how long our reach is, and you'd be right in assuming that we'd use that reach in this situation," Free said.

"Okay, so where is she?" I asked.

"Mexico," Destiny replied.

"And where is my husband?" I asked.

"En route to Mexico," Angel replied.

I swiftly put the remaining pieces of the puzzle together, and now, I knew what his note meant.

He was doing what I asked, and I knew that he was more than capable of standing on business, but I still felt the twinges of fear in my heart. Nobody could stand up against a well-placed bullet, not even someone with the last name Walker.

"What's his plan?" I asked.

Nobody verbally responded, but all eyes were on me.

"Okay, so even if he kills her, what happens to her baby?"

"It's cute that you would show concern for a woman who vowed to kill your baby," Angel said.

"That baby is innocent, and you know that. My concern ain't for her; it's for my nephew, and I'm sure that you can understand that seeing as how you weren't all in agreement to kill Royal once upon a time," I replied.

The way Angel's eyes flashed told me that I'd hit a nerve, but Free kept that neutral expression that seemed unshakable.

"We've dealt with the tests that came with our family, so if I were you, I'd stay focused on yours right now," Destiny advised.

"What's that supposed to mean?" I asked defensively.

"What's your next move?" Free asked.

The immediate anger that took ahold of me was because I felt like I was being played with, and if these bitches thought that was okay, then they had me fucked up. The only thing that held my tongue was the memory of the conversation that I'd just had with these same women yesterday. If I didn't know better, I would've thought that they knew about my twin before we had the conversation about family loyalty, but I wasn't about to be that paranoid. This was simply bad timing or the devil's sense of humor. Either way, I had a decision to make.

"My next move is to contact David," I said.

"Explain that," Angel said, smirking.

"David is the Captain Save-A-Hoe type all the way to his soul, so if we let him know what's going on, then he'll come to his son's rescue at the very least. Tynesha will just be the battery in his back," I replied logically.

"So, you want to use your nephew, your INNOCENT nephew, as bait against his father?" Free asked.

"Yep," I stated unflinchingly.

Destiny chuckled, and Angel's smirk only got wider.

"That's ruthless," Destiny said.

"That's her Walker side showing," Angel said.

"To answer your earlier question, Stormy is with Madeline and the rest of the other kids, and we're with you," Free said.

"I really appreciate that, but... I gotta do this without you. David has to die by my hand since the blood of Tynesha will be on the hands of my husband. Him and I are in this together. I don't mind you all supporting both of us from the shadows, but the bottom line is that we gotta put our own work in out here," I replied genuinely.

They all shared a look that I couldn't decipher, but no one objected to what I was saying.

"So, what do you need?" Destiny asked.

Her question caused me to pace the length of the room as I contemplated the most strategic move in order to achieve my ultimate goal. I knew that it didn't make sense for me to go to Mexico because that would only distract Royal and make him feel like he had to protect me. I needed to think outside the box, and as soon as that thought crossed my mind, I could feel the makings of something diabolical stretching the corners of my imagination.

"Does David know where Ty and her son are at the moment?" I asked, coming to stand back behind Destiny.

"There's really no way for me to know that because his passport hasn't been stamped in Mexico, but that doesn't mean shit. Your twin's passport wasn't stamped either. She just happened to move through territory where we have alliances and eyes on the street," Destiny replied.

"Okay, so let's assume that he got word that Ty crossed into Mexico, which means that we need to reroute him and focus his attention somewhere else," I reasoned.

"How do you suggest doing that?" Angel asked.

My mind flashed back to an accidental trick that me and my twin had played on David the first time he came to dinner at my mom's house. He hadn't known that I wasn't Tynesha, and I took advantage of that by sucking his dick til his soul left his body. That was the beginning of the end.

"David can't tell me and my twin apart, so all I have to do is show up somewhere that he would expect to see me," I said.

"You wanna go to Florida?" Free asked.

The smile that I gave her was bright and completely mischievous.

"This bitch is up to no good," Angel said, wagging her finger at me.

"Maybe a little, but nah, I ain't trying to pop up in Florida because I've got a hidden agenda. I know that David, me, and my mom did our dirt, but that was between us and God, and that's how it should've stayed. There was a Judas in the family though," I said, tasting hatred bubbling within the saliva coating my mouth.

"Your cousin?" Destiny asked.

"You wanna go to Africa," Free quickly deduced.

When my eyes locked with hers, I saw the lights of pleasure mirrored back at me, and she gave me a slight nod.

"David wouldn't expect your twin to show up on his doorstep, not after what she did by fucking with Roland," Angel said.

"Not unless she was desperate, running for her life, and betting that David would spare her life for their child's sake," Free said, reading my mind exactly.

"Okay, but what if he doesn't think that you're her?" Destiny asked.

"Rational thought won't be possible because all he'll be thinking about is one of us being in the same location as Shaomi," I replied.

My statement was met by approving silence that only bolstered my feelings about this working, and that had me mentally ready for war.

"Let me make a call," Free said, stepping out of the room.

"I gotta admit, Tesha, this is a bold ass move, but it's well played on your part," Angel said.

"I'm glad that you approve, but I need you to keep Royal in the dark about what my play is because he needs to concentrate," I requested.

"You know that we don't keep secrets," Destiny replied.

"I get that, and I'll tell him as soon as the time is right, but not right now," I vowed.

I could tell by the look that they shared that they were more than a little uneasy with what I was asking of them, but they could still understand the logic. After a few moments, they nodded reluctantly, and that was when Free came back into the room.

"Aight, so, I had Madeline reach out to a few friends of hers in Africa, and they agreed to let you catch a ride on a military transport plane. This keeps your entry into the country off anyone's radar, and you can use Royal's resources after you touch down. It's leaving in less than an hour though so grab whatever you need, and we'll drop you off," Free said.

"Do I need weapons?" I asked.

"Nah, you'll be given a few toys to aide in your mission, plus I know my little brother has a gun or two hidden on his compound," Free replied.

"Okay, then. I just need to grab my shoes and phone. I'll meet you all downstairs," I said, quickly leaving the room and heading back to my bedroom.

Even though I knew that the weather would be warm in Africa, I still traded my shorts for a pair of Black Billionaire, khaki, capri pants, and I stepped into my matching thigh high Black Billionaire leather boots. When I grabbed my phone off of the nightstand, I noticed a text message from Royal, and I quickly opened it. The two word message of 'stay safe' made me question the decision I'd made to keep him in the dark, and I realized that I wasn't willing to start our marriage with lies. I hurriedly texted him my next move as I headed downstairs and out front to the idling Range Rover.

"You ready for this, Tesha?" Angel asked.

"Don't let the pretty face fool you, sis. I been with the shits," I replied, smiling.

Chapter 10

(Royal) (Mexico)

Fluency in languages had become one of my hobbies in the last five years, and it served me well right now as the men spoke to me in rapid fire Spanish. I wasn't happy with the shit that they were telling me, but I kept my displeasure to myself, and I kept my eyes out the window of the speeding gray Bronco we were travelling in. When my eyes flickered to the passenger side mirror, I saw the small blue Toyota pickup and the green Toyota 4runner still right behind us with guns visible. The constant drug wars made Mexico look and feel like a middle eastern warzone, but this wasn't anything that I hadn't seen in other countries on other continents. Cartels had the power in Mexico, which was why my family was aligned with that power source, and I had the ability to hunt out here like it was the African safari.

With the moves I'd made and the money I'd spent while en route, I'd expected to find Tynesha with a bright red ribbon tied around her, but apparently, that was too much to ask for. She'd given my associates the slip, leaving a consolation prize in the form of the helper she'd had to make it this far. Hopefully, that person had enough information to save their own life. I pulled my phone out to text Destiny to see if there was anything new that she could tell me, but I resisted the urge to text my wife and check on her. I respected the fact that she told me the truth, and the only way that I knew how to show the appreciation for that respect was to not micromanage her actions. I knew that Tesha could handle her own and get down with the baddest muthafuckas, so all I could really do was trust her to handle the business.

As the Bronco came to a stop in front of a rundown building, I got a response from Destiny that nothing new had come across her screen, and the Feds still weren't looking in the direction of Mexico for Ty's whereabouts. I pocketed my phone, hopped out of the truck, and followed Juan-Carlos inside the building. A long time ago, this place had probably been a small factory, but from the moment that I entered, all I could sense and smell was death all around. It reminded me of the hospital in Florida. Juan-Carlos led me across the open floor to the back of the makeshift warehouse, stopping outside of a blacked-out cubicle.

"Turn on the lights," I instructed.

A few seconds later, the cubicle lit up, and I saw a naked woman chained spread eagle on the floor. She was covered in blood and beat the fuck up, but she was alive. Barely. As soon as I walked in the door, I could hear her breathing, and it was a wet rattling sound, like she was drawing air into broken lungs full of blood. Her left eye was swollen shut, but her right eye still showed signs of being alert as it slowly searched my face. It was obvious that she'd once been a beautiful woman, but from the looks of things, she'd been turned into a human piñata.

"Where's Ty?" I asked calmly.

"K-Kill me. Please," she begged in a voice just above a strangled whisper.

"I asked you a question, and I asked it nicely, so you should probably answer before my tone changes," I warned.

"I-I don't know where she is. I s-swear."

In Spanish, Juan-Carlos told me that this lady was named Vanessa, and she was a truck driver from Texas. She'd brought Ty and her baby across the border and dropped them off in Mexico City. At least that was the story that she was sticking to.

"Kill me please," the woman begged again, sobbing openly.

The tears that I saw leaking out of her good eye, and from beneath her swollen eye lid, had the stench of desperation and defeat. I'd seen this before, and it was a sure sign that this was a broken woman before me. Despite me being here to do a job, something about this truth left me with a feeling of unease in the pit of my stomach. Ever since I'd gotten to Russia with Tesha, I'd been living a life that was full, even though I'd suppressed my desire to kill, and now, I was wondering if that desire had vanished. Had I somehow lost the taste for the savage rules of the game that guaranteed survival for the Apex predators? And if I had, what would that mean for my family's survival? I knew that I couldn't afford to find out, especially not right now, so I closed that part of my mind and refocused on the task at hand. I asked Juan-Carlos if they had picked up this supposed drop off on camera anywhere, and he quickly reminded me that this wasn't the United States with one hundred cameras on every block. That meant that the foot work would have to be done the old-fashioned way, but a beautiful American woman with a baby wasn't something that blended in well.

"Take me to Mexico City," I demanded, turning for the door.

"W-Wait! Please," Vanessa begged.

When I looked back at her, an odd question popped into my mind, and suddenly, I felt the weight of my gun in my hand. If this was a woman that I loved, what would I have the man in my position do?

"There are fates worse than death... but you don't deserve them," I said, raising my pistol slightly.

"Thank you," she sighed.

Her eye never left mine as I squeezed the trigger once, causing the .45 to jump within my grip. Instantly, the light went out inside her, and I felt something similar inside myself, but I ignored it.

"Now, take me to Mexico City," I demanded before heading back outside.

When I got back inside the Bronco, I texted Destiny and told her to look through any and all security footage that she could access in Mexico City. They might not have cameras like the U.S., but they weren't so archaic as to have absolutely zero security precautions in their major cities, especially not with cartel issues.

"You need to know that Mexico City is not controlled by the Juarez Cartel, so we will be riding into enemy territory," Juan-Carlos stated.

"You're not afraid, are you, Juan?" I asked, glancing over at him.

His laughter was genuine, and then, he started spitting rapid fire instructions to his men over the two-way phone in his hand before he started the truck and pulled off. My focus went back to my phone, and this time, I did check in with Tesha, just to let her know which direction I was headed in. She hit me back immediately and let me know that she'd be touching down at my compound in Nigeria to gather supplies, and then, she'd make the hop to Ghana. After giving her my love, I checked in with my pops to see how Stormy was doing, and he sent me a picture of him with my younger siblings mixed in with the grandchildren surrounding him on the couch. This made me laugh out loud because I knew that my pops was a gangster by all definitions of the word, but that nigga was bubble gum soft when it came to the kids. They had him wrapped around their little fingers, and it reminded me of how Vito was in *The Godfather Part II*. I loved seeing my dad like this though, especially because I knew how much he'd missed out on in all of his grown kids' lives. He gave me hope that gangsters could actually retire and live the dream of actually watching their families grow from generation to generation. I sent him a message, telling him to kiss my baby, and then, I put my mind back on the task at hand. Since there wasn't a lot that I could really do at the moment, I made the arrangements for a private plane to fly me and my passengers out of Mexico City. Once that was done, I made sure to send my yacht home. The plan was to drop Ty where she stood, grab the baby, and vanish. I would decide what to do next after consulting with my wife because the last thing that I wanted was to do something that would forever drive a wedge between her and I. My family was my reason for existing, and I would hold on to that with a death grip.

Half an hour into our journey to Mexico City, I got a text from Destiny with instructions to watch the video attached. When I did, I saw Ty walking into a glass, high-rise building with her son in her arms and a backpack on her back.

"Take me here," I said, showing the frozen image of the building to Juan-Carlos.

He looked at my screen, looked back at the road, looked back at my screen, and then, he shook his head no.

"What the fuck do you mean no?" I asked in Spanish to make sure that my displeasure wasn't lost in translation.

"We cannot go into that building, Jefe. It will start a war."

"How? I'm not saying that we have to announce our presence or anything. All we gotta do is go in, kill her, and leave," I explained patiently.

"You don't understand. You come into town for a few hours, start some shit, and then leave us to finish it. What you do will make us a target."

"Okay, well, that's why you're well paid in money and drugs, ese, so I don't see the problem," I replied.

"Of course you don't see the problem. You're a spoiled ass miyate American," he said under his breath.

My body instantly went cold at his use of the Spanish word for nigger, and I had to resist the urge to knock his muthafuckin brains out the window with a bullet from my gun. I tried counting to ten, but I only made it halfway before I opened my mouth again.

"Do you wanna call your patron or should I?"

The glare that he gave me out of the corner of his eye let me know how much he really hated me in this moment, and I filed that away for later because I was definitely going to kill him for it. He took a few seconds to pick his phone up and let his men know over the two-way that we were headed to the Devil's Lair. I would've believed that he was exaggerating for dramatic effect were it not for the immediate response of cussing and yelling about how crazy this shit was. I'd been joking earlier when I'd asked Juan-Carlos if he was scared, but it was looking like that was a joke that carried a lot of truth. It was on the tip of my tongue to recommend a change of career for this group of supposedly trained hittas, but I kept quiet. The rest of the ride to Mexico City was one full of tension and awkward silence, but I damn sure wasn't about to be the nigga to fix a bitch ass thing. This shit here was grown man business and coddling a nigga was what we were NOT about to do. When we finally pulled up to the building, I quickly dismissed the thoughts of Juan-Carlos' feelings, and I put my mind back on what I'd came here for.

"I'mma go in here and toss some money around to see if we can handle this quietly. Wait here," I said, hopping out of the truck and walking like I was born just up the block from here.

When I walked into the lobby, the smell of money was permeating the air, and I knew that cash was the only thing that these people wanted to talk about. I pulled my billfold out of my pocket as I approached the front desk, already locking eyes with the sexy, dark-haired Latina standing behind the desk.

"How are you doing, beautiful? I'm looking for..."

"The exit is right behind you and have a nice day, sir," she said in flawless English with a slight accent.

Her abrupt, abrasive response caught me off guard, and I could literally feel my mouth hanging open in shock.

"Listen, I'm just trying to conduct a little business..."

"Then you're obviously in the wrong place because you don't have any business here in this building," she replied smoothly.

"Money talks, sweetheart, and if you want me to be honest, I know that I can buy this building and everything in it, including you," I said, smirking.

"Somehow, I doubt that. Now, I advise you to leave."

"You doubt that, huh? Well, just tell me who owns the building and watch me close escrow before your lunch break," I vowed seriously.

"Sir, if you don't know who owns this building, then you are most definitely in the wrong place, so I suggest you get the fuck out."

Her tone had switched to the polite nastiness that seemed to be a trademark of anyone who worked customer service. I could ignore her tone and keep pushing, but there was something about the look in her eyes that tapped into the warning bells that were suddenly sounding in my brain. Without another word, I put my money back in my pocket, nodded at her, and turned to leave. During the entire walk back across the lobby, my eyes stayed on a swivel, looking for the slightest thing that could be viewed as a threat. I didn't see anything, but when I made it to the front door, my heart dropped to my socks at the sight before me. The roundabout in front of the building, where I'd pulled up in a three truck, heavily armed motorcade, was empty, like I'd arrived on foot. I tried not to panic as I looked around, expecting to see that the hittas I'd come with had just moved out of the fire zone or something, but I saw no sign of Juan-Carlos. I was DEFINITELY going to kill his ass for this, but that was a plan for later. I pulled my phone out and texted Destiny so that she could send me a car, and I told her what happened. As soon as I hit the send button, I felt movement behind me, but I never got to turn around before I was hit hard over the head. The next thing I knew, the concrete sidewalk was rushing up at me, and I fell into it like a backyard swimming pool. Then, I lost consciousness.

Chapter 11

(David) (Mexico)

"Uncle Umar, I'm just calling to give you an update. On the plane, I found out that Ty is wanted for killing Roland, but she escaped the net that the cops tried to drop on her. I don't know where she went, but I'm in Veracruz, Mexico trying to plan my next move before I cross the border," I said.

"Well, you've got good fortune on your side because her killing Roland effectively exonerated you for that murder. I've already spoken with my people in Washington D.C. about it, which means that you're not wanted, and you can cross into the U.S. whenever. I have it on good authority though that Ty crossed into Mexico with Rashon and that she's still out there somewhere."

I didn't know if my uncle's words about good fortune were accurate, but I knew that I wasn't playing as far behind the eight ball as I'd anticipated when I'd left Africa. The purpose now had to be utilizing what I knew to take full advantage of all the things that I could exploit. The problem was that I was emotionally all over the place.

"I'm gonna see what I can find out down here. I need you to send me a contact for your people within the Sinola Cartel because I'm gonna need their help too," I said.

"I'm sending it now, nephew. Call me when you have an update, and I will do the same."

"I will," I replied, disconnecting the call.

"So, what's the deal?" Carrie asked from the chair that she was sitting in next to our motel room door.

Calling her had been one of the first things I did when I hopped on the plane because I knew that I could trust her to have my back no matter the situation. She was more than just a beautiful woman with some great pussy. She'd become a loyal friend who had saved me from myself in more ways than one. There was never a doubt in my mind that I'd call her for any battle I was in, even if that meant taking her away from her husband and kids.

"My uncle said that Ty killing Roland has exonerated me, which means they've had to figure out his real identity despite the face job he had done. He also said that Ty crossed into Mexico."

"Does he know where she is?" Carrie asked.

"Nah, he's relying on me to figure that out, which means that I'm relying on you," I replied, reaching for my laptop at the foot of the bed that I was sitting on.

"It ain't as easy as finding a needle in a haystack, is it?"

"Your sarcasm is duly noted, asshole," I replied, chuckling as I shook my head.

"Whatever, you still love me. So, tell me how the life of a king is over there in the Motherland since you ain't invited me over not once in the last year."

"Life is... complicated. And you know why I haven't invited you over," I said, giving her a knowing look.

"Ahhh, you still want this pussy on your face. I get it."

I couldn't help the laughter that bubbled up and burst out of me, but the random thought of Shaomi had a sobering affect that made me stop laughing.

"Shaomi's pregnant again," I said, looking over at her.

"Damn, you don't waste no time, do you? How many kids is this now, eighteen or nineteen?"

"Shut the hell up. You know damn well it ain't that many! And you act like I meant to get her pregnant again when the reality is that we only had sex once... vaginally anyway," I replied.

"Ohhh, she let you plant seeds in her backyard, huh? That woman is trying to make sure that you don't fuck with nobody else because I'mma tell you right now that I don't give up the ass to just anyone. This asshole is sacred, so you gotta be special."

The look that she gave me had some intended heat behind it that made me want to put a little pleasure before business, but I resisted the temptation.

"We'll continue this conversation later," I said, turning my focus back to the laptop in front of me.

"Yeah, I bet we will."

Her laughter had me shaking my head and smiling, but I was determined to stay focused on what was important. The first thing that I did was hack into what passed for the law enforcement database in this part of the world, hoping to get lucky and find some reported sightings. It only took a few minutes to determine that a lost cause, which brought me to my next option of checking border crossings. The last time that I'd checked, Ty didn't have a passport, but a little digging into her life in the last year revealed that she had, in fact, obtained one. It hadn't been swiped or flagged into any country, and she hadn't made it to Interpol's wanted list yet.

"Americans don't necessarily stand out in Mexico like they used to, and with her living in Texas, it would stand to reason that she's learned Spanish," Carrie said.

"Okay, and?"

"So, I don't think that she's moving like an outsider because it makes more sense to blend in with her surroundings," Carrie replied.

I was following her train of thought, and the best way for Ty to blend in was if she had at least one ally in Mexico. Finding that person or persons would lead me straight to her.

"Do you know if she has friends out here?" I asked, looking up from the laptop's screen.

"Not right off hand, but more than likely, she would've made friends of the alliances formed between Texas and here. Didn't you say that the Zeta Cartel was Roland's new best friend?"

"Yeah, but do you really think that Ty would turn to the cartel for help when she knows nobody in that life can be trusted?" I asked skeptically.

"Don't forget how desperate she has to be feeling right now."

I took a moment to factor that into the equation, and it was easy to see how Ty would view her options as no more angels and only demons to choose from. The question now was could I get the Zetas to deal with me? Their loyalty to any outsider could presumably be bought, so it was really just a matter of price. I picked my phone back up, intending to text my uncle and see what type of proposition we could make, but I didn't get that far because a waiting video message alert that I'd missed stopped me cold.

"What's wrong?" Carrie asked.

"Huh?"

"What's wrong, David? You're visibly shaken, so what are you looking at?" she asked, crossing the room and sitting beside me on the bed.

I didn't say anything, only because I couldn't find the words, so I simply showed her my phone's screen. I knew that she would understand the trauma and memory that I was trying to fight through because she'd been with me the night I'd gotten Ty's sex tape of her fucking Roland. I could remember everything that happened that night, but if I was ever asked how I felt, I could only remember being cold. So incredibly cold.

"Do you want me to look at it?" she asked gently, putting her hand on top of mine.

I couldn't find the words to offer up a verbal reply, so I nodded once and allowed the phone to be taken from my hand. My eyes went to her face in hopes of gauging whatever the message was through her features. There was no immediate shock and awe, which gave me some comfort, but she was still looking at the video over and over again.

"What is it?" I finally asked.

"It's her, but it's nothing sexual."

That was all I needed to hear in order to reclaim my phone and watch the video for myself. I thought that Ty would've said something to me, but there was a text message attached instead that said she needed my help, and she was coming to me. I could see a plane behind her, but not the tail number or anything identifiable for me to be able to track her down. She was in a field and not an airport, but that didn't help either.

"What the fuck does she mean that she's coming to me? Has this bitch lost her entire mind?" I asked, completely confused.

"Like I said, she's more than desperate, and you're definitely the evil she knows. No doubt she's probably betting on you not killing her for the sake of your son."

"Not even he can save her life," I stated callously.

I understood that Tynesha was my son's mother, but that bitch would forever be the opp to me, and that was just fine by me.

"Shaomi and I will raise him like we talked about, so he won't really miss Ty..."

"Wait a minute, wait a minute. Are you saying that you and Shaomi have already had that conversation about Tynesha being dead and gone?" Carrie asked.

"Yeah, why wouldn't we?"

"Uh, because she's still your wife, dummy. Or how about the fact that she's still Shaomi's fucking blood cousin?" she asked.

"All that shit is irrelevant at this point, so ain't no need wasting time with this argument."

"David, I fuck with you the long way, and I ain't trying to argue, but you're not looking at this straight. I mean, just think about it for a moment. What bitch do you know that's just gonna be cool with you killing their muthafuckin family? Especially family that they grew up with? Then, you gotta think about how fucking messy Shaomi has been in all of this because she masterminded the exposure of everybody's secrets. Shit, if she would've known about me and you, I'm sure that shit would've got aired out too," she said.

"I hear you, but Shaomi was just putting the truth out there to hurt Ty because she knew that Ty had hurt me by lying. Shaomi just had my back in this fight."

"That might be part of her motivation, but from where I'm sitting, it don't just look like Shaomi wanted to get even for your pain. She wanted what Ty had, and she wanted to avenge her own pain as well," she stated calmly.

I checked my instinctive desire to respond and just took a moment to contemplate what was being suggested to me right now. I'd known Shaomi for years, and I knew that she had no problems going for hers, but to intentionally destroy her own family was farfetched. It was plausible but not probable.

"I understand that Ty is your friend, Carrie, and your loyalty is to her, but I..."

"Hold up. You're right. Ty is my girl, but my loyalty ain't in question right now because if we keeping it one hundred, then you should know that my loyalty is to you first. I've only put my life in *your* hands. That should tell you that what I'm telling you is only because I want what's best for you and your soul, not because of Ty and definitely not because of your queen in Africa," she said in a voice comprised of anger and hurt.

I reached for her hand, intending to pull her toward me so that I could apologize, but I was frozen in midair by a sudden terrifying thought.

"She-She said that she was coming to me," I mumbled, hurriedly dialing the number that she'd sent the message from.

"Yeah, she did..."

"You don't understand, Carrie. If she's coming to me, then we've got a big fucking issue. She can't know that I'm in Mexico because I just got here, so..."

"She's headed for Africa," Carrie said, finishing my thought.

I put the phone to my ear and listened helplessly as it rang over and over again. I finally hung up and called right back, but the results didn't change, and I could feel the panic on a steady rise working its way up my toes.

"We gotta go," I said, hanging up again and immediately calling to make sure that my family's plane was fueled and ready to taxi.

"Go? Go where?"

"Back to Africa! Think about it, Carrie. If you just sat here and analyzed Shaomi's actions through the perspective that you did, then what the fuck has Ty been thinking and feeling? By your own words, Shaomi took what she wanted, and now she's pregnant again. What would you do?"

"Oh, shit," she said, getting off the bed and grabbing the overnight bag that she'd come with.

Once I got off the phone with the pilot, I tried calling Shaomi five times back-to-back, but she didn't answer.

"I'll drive," Carrie said, opening the door and leading the way outside.

I quickly hopped in the passenger seat of her gun metal gray Dodge Ram 1500 as my fingers were already hitting the redial button. When I got no answer again, I hung up and tried calling my uncle, who thankfully answered on the fourth ring.

"Uncle Umar, Tynesha is headed for Ghana!"

"What? Why would you think that she's coming out here to Africa?" he asked, confused.

"I don't have time to explain. I just need you to lock the compound down."

"David, it is not as simple as that. I'm in a meeting right now away from the main house, but still on the property. Shaomi is sleep, and the kids are all running around the compound. A lockdown takes time."

"Then do it now instead of arguing! I don't know how much of a head start Ty has, but she could be there anytime," I said with mounting aggravation.

"Fine, nephew. I'll..."

The resounding click that I heard in my ear let me know that the call was over, but the fact that he'd been in mid-sentence told me that it wasn't voluntarily ended. I quickly dialed his number back, but it didn't ring once. There was just a busy signal blaring back at me. My instincts told me to try to call Shaomi back, and when I did, I was rewarded with the same busy signal.

"Get us to the airport now," I demanded, still trying in vain to get through to anyone in my house.

"David, what's going on?"

"All I'm getting is a busy signal," I replied.

"What do you think that is?" she asked, reaching for my hand.

I looked over at her and said a silent prayer that I was wrong.

"I think someone is jamming the signal to cause interference with the cell service out there, and if that's the case, then the odds are good that it's Tynesha. That means she's within striking distance of my compound, and no one there is ready."

Chapter 12

(Tynesha) (Mexico City)

The smells of delicious food wafted on the air, testing my stomach's resilience as well as my good manners because I really wanted to get up and go find the source of the aromas punching me. I dared not move though. I'd been sitting on the black, leather sofa, enjoying the view from the penthouse, awaiting the appointment that I was promised when I'd called for help. I was waiting on the defacto leader of the Zeta Cartel, known only as Red Devil. When it came to his business dealings with the cartel, it was impossible for Roland to keep shit a secret from me, especially because he loved to pillow talk of his dreams to be the next Sosa. Me knowing that I was only with him for as long as he proved to be useful was the reason that I'd listened to his ramblings, but it turned out to help me and my son. I knew that the knowledge that I'd amassed could make the Zeta Cartel an ally, so as soon as we crossed into Mexico, I began laying the foundation for my next move.

Roland had learned a thing or two from his dealings with Zoe Pound, meaning that he finally learned the lessons about trusting a family that he wasn't a part of. He wouldn't do that dumb shit twice, which was why he created an escape plan from his dealings with the cartel from the jump, and naturally, he told me all about it. He'd begun stealing dope and money, hiding it in a place only he or I could get to, but in my heart, I'd always known that he'd done too much to earn my forgiveness. Even if he had infinite lifetimes to atone for shit, it wouldn't have mattered because the hate I felt was real. For that reason, I'd been stealing from him, creating my own stash separate from his stolen goods to make sure that me and Rashon would be good no matter what. I'd robbed that nigga blind, so his stash was a great bargaining chip because it was insignificant for real. When I'd contacted Red Devil, I'd told her all about Roland's betrayal and where to find his stash. All I asked for in return was for her help to make it out of Mexico alive and not in law enforcement custody.

The deal that we'd struck was contingent upon my information leading to what I'd promised, which was why I'd been locked up tight in her penthouse like a princess in a fairy tale. She'd told me to relax and keep her abuela company, but it was hard to relax when a three man team of hired hittas was constantly roaming around her spot with machine guns in their grip. These niggas stayed on ten! Rashon was blissfully asleep, such as the innocence of a child would allow, but my muthafuckin eyeballs were glued open, waiting for some shit to pop off. I'd told the truth about what I knew, but there was always the off chance that Roland had gotten paranoid and moved his stash. All I could do was wait and see. One of the gunmen coming around the corner and into the living room got my attention because he was moving with a purposeful stride. He walked right past me without a glance in my direction, heading farther back into the penthouse, but returned seconds later with two other men in tow. They left the apartment clearly on a mission, and even though I had no idea what was going on, I still got a knot in my stomach the size of a cantaloupe. My mind was so busy running through scenarios that I didn't even see the tiny Spanish lady enter the room with a plate piled high with food in her hands. She smiled at me, pushed the plate into my hands, and then left without uttering a single word. My rational mind was telling me how impolite it would be not to eat, especially because this was someone's abuela's cooking, but the big bitch in me already had the fork in my hand. I recognized the beans, rice, and corn tortillas, but the meat was an unknown. I tasted a little piece at first, and that shit was so good that I had to close my eyes while I chewed slow. After that, I was like a dog off the leash, fucking shit up with no remorse or regard for human life. I hadn't eaten in a while, but I couldn't even blame my inhalation of the food on that because the shit was just good as fuck. By the time I got down to the last of my four corn tortillas, I got the feeling of being watched, and I looked up to find Red Devil standing a few feet away from me. My fork froze in midair.

"Please continue to eat. It's good, no?"

"It's amazing," I said, holding my hand up to my mouth so that I wouldn't accidentally spit food out of my mouth.

"I know. My abuela is the best cook I've ever known. Even better than me mama. I try to tell her to rest and save her strength, but she enjoys nothing more than cooking and feeding people."

"She should have her own restaurant," I commented.

"I agree, and I even tried to buy for her, but she refuses to share her recipes with anyone outside of the family. She says that they are part of her soul, and therefore they must be protected."

"She sounds like a very passionate and wise person," I said, still eating.

"Si. The passion is in her blood, like it is mine, but I gave up cooking because it stopped bringing me joy."

"Why did it stop bringing you joy?" I asked curiously.

For a moment, she didn't speak, and her eyes got a far off look in them that I recognized as what people looked like when they were reminiscing. I said nothing to interrupt her because I wanted to be respectful of whatever special moment in time had her captured, but when her eyes focused on me, all I saw was an inferno of hate. Her eyes flickered to my son before returning to my face, and I could see a deep sadness circling the madness around the brown in her eyes.

"I used to love cooking with my son. From the time he was three years old, I had him in the kitchen with me, singing old songs I'd learned as a girl back in Columbia. It was perfect, even though it was just the two of us for the most part. He was my world, and everything in it, so it was only natural that I share my love of cooking with him. By the time he was seven years old, he could cook almost as good as me, but I always told him that he was better because I knew in my heart that he would be one day. That day never came though."

"Why not?" I asked before I could stop myself from crossing that line between curious and downright nosy.

"I lost him... A little more than a year ago, he was taken from me."

Her revelation rendered me silent, and all of a sudden, the food that I was chewing didn't taste as delicious as before. I sat the plate on the coffee table in front of me and looked to my left at the peacefulness that was my baby boy. I couldn't imagine or entertain the thought of losing him, and for damn sure not to unnatural causes. I wasn't dumb enough or insensitive enough to ask for details about her son, but the way that she'd put it sounded like her son's death came at the hands of another. The sound of the front door opening, followed by rapidly moving feet, interrupted the awkward moment, and I was thankful that she was forced to turn her attention to more pressing matters. One of her men came in and started speaking in Spanish at the speed of chopper bullets. I could understand what he was saying; it just took me a little while to let my brain catch up to the translation. The first part of his message brought me relief because they had found the half a million dollars and eight kilos of fentanyl that Roland had buried. The rest of what he said gave me cause for concern because, apparently, someone had arrived on the premises uninvited, looking for someone. It wasn't said who he was looking for, but they'd knocked ole boy out and tied him up so that they could ask him some questions. My nerves were standing on edge now, and I started looking around the apartment for the fastest route of escape just in case this had anything to do with me.

"You are safe. Wait here," she instructed before she followed her man out of the room.

My instincts were screaming at me that this was a bad fucking idea, but the reality of my situation was that I wouldn't get far without this woman's help. I needed her, so that meant I needed to chill the fuck out and just wait. The sight of Rashon stirring awake from his nap was the perfect distraction that I needed, and I immediately picked him up. I gave him kisses all over his face until he was wide awake, and then, I went about changing his diaper. By the time I had all of that done, I knew that his little fat ass was hungry and about to act a fool, so I carried him and his bottle with me into the kitchen. Abuela was still whipping up a storm, but when I asked her if I could use the microwave, she graciously moved over and allowed me to get to it. After I got his formula warmed up, I took him back into the living room where I sat and fed him.

"Don't you be greedy either, fat man. You take your time," I said, smiling because of the way his eyes lit up once the bottle was in motion.

His smile never wavered as his big lips latched on the nipple, and he got active with consumption. The way that his little fists pumped the air like he was trying to fly and drink at the same time had me laughing out loud, which delighted him more. When I heard the front door open, I looked up toward the hallway, and when Red Devil came back around the corner, my laughter died instantly. It wasn't the gun in her hand or the blood stains on her white summer dress. It was the half-crazed look in her eyes. It was a look of extreme focus and unspeakable joy, bordering on bloodlust.

"Uh, are you good?" I asked slowly.

"Oh, I'm great. I'm better than great, and I have you to thank for it."

"Me? What do you mean?" I asked cautiously.

Right about now would be the moment when I slipped my gun into my hand, just to have the comfort that it provided, but logic told me that any movement could be perceived as a hostile act, especially that one.

"The man who came here is looking for you, and he claims to be your friend."

"I seriously doubt that because the only muthafuckas looking for me are my opps and law enforcement, so whoever he is, I don't know him," I replied confidently.

"I do not care if he is your friend. I only care that he is my enemy that I've dreamed of taking my revenge on. So, I have you to thank for that gift."

"Okay, well, you're welcome... But why do I get the feeling that there's more?" I asked, repositioning Rashon so that my palm was resting on the butt of my gun.

"More you say? Well, the more is my curiosity at this point. On the elevator ride back up here, I kept asking myself why he was here, on territory that he is not familiar with, looking for his American friend and her baby. Then, I thought about your baby, your beautiful little nino, and a stranger question crossed my mind."

"What question?" I asked after she stood there silently, looking at Rashon.

"I was wondering who his father is?"

My stomach took a turn so fast that I was certain that my son was going to be wearing abuela's cuisine at any second, but I held it in. Never in my wildest dreams did I consider that David would come for me, or at least not without me calling for help, but her question now had his face embedded on my brain. I had no doubt that David could've made an enemy out of this woman, but goddamn, I didn't want it to be true.

"My-My son's father isn't in this country or North America, so I'm sure that's not who you have downstairs," I replied, fighting against the shakiness in my voice.

"Oh, of that I'm quite sure. But you know, when I first saw your nino, I had a strange feeling of déjà vu, like I'd seen him before, but I knew that was impossible because he's just a baby. It wasn't until I bumped into my old enemy downstairs that I got the idea that I might know your son's father. So, who is he? And please keep your hands where I can see them," she said, raising her pistol and cocking it.

Before I could even react to the pistol inches from my face, Abuela stepped from around the corner, holding a double barrel, 12 gauge, sawed off shotgun, and she meant business. My head was spinning, screaming at me that what I was seeing was not actually happening right now. The look on her grandma's face said that she was with all the shits though.

"Listen, whatever my baby daddy did has nothing to do with me and my son, so please don't hurt us," I begged without shame.

"His name?" she asked again.

"David. His name is David Bishop," I replied.

My words made her smile, but inside, I was already crying because her look told me just how bad I'd misjudged this ally.

"I don't know your son's father, but I met him once. He descended on my house under the cover of darkness, killing anyone who stood between him and his target. He came for my son's father. He came for Viktor, but his actions cost me my son, Paco. So, tell me why should I spare you or your son when that same mercy wasn't given to me?"

Chapter 13

(Tesha) (Ghana)

On the day that Roland had shot me down like a dog in the street and left me to die, my twin and I had been preparing to celebrate our birthday. After that, we were jetting off to Africa to pop up on her husband in secret, but in order to do that, she'd had to find out just where he was located. Time had passed and my bullet wounds had long healed, but I hadn't forgotten shit, which was why I was able to creep up on David's family estate undetected. Madeline's people had supplied me with a few military toys, including a prototypical, one-piece catsuit that was completely bulletproof up to 30mm rounds. The moment that I'd put it on, I felt invincible, on some superhero type shit, but I remained focused on the task at hand. In Nigeria, I'd picked up a party of ten men who'd all sworn their allegiance to Royal a long time ago, and they would accompany me on my mission. I didn't know if we'd be outnumbered, but logically, I figured that David's Uncle Umar had no reason to feel like a threat could touch any of them out here. As soon as the two Jeeps that we were travelling in got within half a mile of David's compound, I sent a few men to check for any soldiers hidden, making sure they used the infrared binoculars, so they missed nothing.

When they reported back to me, I was told of only a handful of guards playing soccer in a field visible from the front of the property and kids running around playing. It was dusk outside, which meant that night would fall sooner than later and give us the advantage. I sent a message to Destiny, letting her know where I was at and what the situation was looking like, and then, I asked her if David had seen the video that I'd sent to his phone from my stop in Nigeria. I'd routed it through Destiny first so that she could put a tracker on it to see when it was opened, but according to her, so far it hadn't been. All we could do was wait. While I'd been en route to Africa, Destiny had found out that David was, in fact, in Mexico, but he hadn't made any noise yet, which meant he probably didn't know where Tynesha was. I could only hope to keep it that way because I didn't need him to bump into Royal and possibly have the upper hand. I had no doubt that if either Ty or David saw Royal, they would know that he meant to kill them both, and they'd join forces in order to cheat death. I wasn't trying to let that happen, and definitely not at the expense of my husband, so I was mentally ready to do anything I could to draw David's attention back to Africa. I was ready to fight, but for the moment, the only thing that I could fight was my own fucking impatience. That all changed the moment that my phone rang, and I saw that it was David trying to call because that automatically meant that he'd seen the video. I shot Destiny a text, telling her to wait a few minutes and then jam the signal for the surrounding five miles. I knew that this would put me out of contact with everybody, but it would work to my overall advantage. I waited in silence until I saw my phone flatline in terms of reception, and then, I took hold of the AR-15 diamondback in my lap.

"Let's go. Don't kill any of the children. We take the guards first," I instructed.

Once the message was passed along, we pulled off in the Jeeps at a slow creep until we could see the mansion in the distance. Not wanting to give any type of warning for our imminent attack had us pull over and make the rest of the journey on foot. By the time we got to the gate, I could still hear the children playing, but there was shouting going on that had a feeling of urgency in the air.

"They know we're coming," a man said from behind me.

"Kill em all," I replied, raising my gun and shooting the two guards occupying the gatehouse out front.

We fanned out and quickly descended on the property with the sounds of bullets making our presence known. Once I made it through the gates, I could tell that the kids didn't know what was going on because they were still running around, playing without a care in the world. I waited until I was closer to them, and then, I raised my gun straight up into the air while firing off several shots.

"Everyone inside. Now!" I yelled.

They immediately started scurrying in a blind panic, but my attention had already shifted toward the group of men and women spilling out of a small, one room house a few feet away. I immediately recognized Umar, and the fact that he still had his phone clutched in his grip led me to the conclusion that someone had given him a heads up. Between the shadows of night and the baklava covering majority of my features, I knew that he wouldn't know the difference between me and my twin. This was my advantage, and I walked right up to him without fear.

"It's been a while, Uncle Umar, but you haven't aged a bit. Did my husband tell you that I was coming?" I asked.

"What do you want? You obviously know that David is not here, nor is he your husband," Umar replied.

"That really hurts, Umar, especially considering that you performed the ceremony which bound us for lifetimes to come," I said.

To my surprise, Umar began to laugh rather loudly, which was way out of place with the seriousness of what was going on here, but I waited for him to finish. Once he had himself back under control, I looked at him before I raised my AR and shot the man who'd been standing a few feet away from him.

"Is this still funny, Uncle?" I asked.

"It is, but I'm afraid that you misunderstand the source of my amusement right now," he replied.

"Do I? Well, why don't you tell me what was so funny because it cost a man his life?" I stated unapologetically.

"It's funny that you say I performed your wedding ceremony because I didn't."

"Huh?" I mumbled.

My mind was immediately wondering if I'd played my hand wrong, or had I somehow got the facts wrong that Ty told me about her wedding to David? I didn't panic though.

"I said that I did not marry you to anyone, Tesha. I only married my nephew to your twin sister, Tynesha. It was funny to me that you thought you could come here and pretend to be her. Even in the dark, I still have eyes, child, as do you, and I looked into Tynesha's eyes enough to know her soul when I saw it again. You may be twins, but your souls will never be the same."

Shock and anger took a hold of me like sister tornadoes spinning across the flats of Oklahoma. I wanted to shoot this old nigga, but in the back of my mind, I knew that he'd be worth more to me alive than dead. Without a word, I raised the AR again, only this time, I struck him with the butt of it in the center of his forehead. He collapsed like an asthmatic after a long race, falling to the ground in a comical, slow-motion fashion.

"Take him to the Jeep and kill the rest," I ordered, turning and heading for the main house.

As I approached the front, I noticed the huge double doors to the house were wide open, which was just another sign to me that Shaomi was too comfortable with her life now, the life that she'd destroyed others for, including the relationship between my twin and our dearly departed mother. After all Shaomi had done, there was no way conceivable to me that she could keep living her best life, and I would burn this whole muthafucka to the ground to prove my point. I crept through the doorway with the AR-15 at my shoulder, ready to work, keeping my eyes on a swivel like windshield wipers in the rain. There were four men accompanying me, and I waved them in different directions so that we could cover more ground faster. I followed the sound of children, which led me to the veranda in the back of the house. As soon as I stepped outside, I saw Shaomi surrounded by half a dozen kids that I'd run off the front lawn, cradling a newborn baby boy in her arms.

"Looks just like his daddy, don't he?" she asked, smiling.

"Thank God," I replied.

"Come on, cuzzo. Don't be like that. Don't be a sore loser in this game because I only did what you told me to do."

"How the fuck do you figure that?" I asked, feeling my anger mounting.

"Remember that conversation we had in David's living room when I confronted you about stealing the love of my life? I believe that your exact words were, 'did I actually leave the love of my life alone for a bitch to take.' Does that ring a bell?"

"Uh huh," I lied, hoping to keep her talking until we had her surrounded on all sides.

"Okay, good. The other thing that you told me was that I had to take what I wanted... So, that's what I did. I took your husband, fucked him, sucked him, and had his baby again. Sorry, not sorry, cousin."

"I didn't come here expecting your trifling ass to be sorry because I know that you're incapable of remorse. The only thing that I wanna know is why you had to destroy our family along the way?" I asked sincerely.

"How else could I have accomplished all of this? Were you really gonna bow out and abdicate the throne to me and my kids? Nah, I don't think so, which is why I had to play for keeps. I'm sure that you understand though, right?" she asked, smiling maliciously at me.

I wanted to give her another hole to breathe out of, but I still didn't see my men coming to help, and I could feel that she was holding something back. She was too smug, too confident, with admitting how she'd played her own family over some dick and some status in this world. I knew bitches who would do more for less, but it was the flaunting of it all that wasn't making sense to me right now. For real, the bitch was talking like I wouldn't shoot her muthafuckin ass right here, right now.

"Any last words, hoe?" I asked, dropping my finger down on the trigger in preparation.

"For you, Tynesha, yeah. I got two words so listen closely. I'm pregnant."

"Bullshit," I blurted instinctively.

Her laughter was immediate, and it was full of confidence that made my stomach turn in a literal way. My trigger finger was itching, but I held still and tried to think about my options.

"I can see your brain working, cousin, and if you really want me to prove my truth, then we can run into town and get a pregnancy test. Of course, you might run into Umar's men along the way and end up dead before you can verify how fertile I really am."

"I'm not too worried about Umar or his men because that problem has already been taken care of. The only thing that I'm really contemplating is whether to shoot you in the head or if I wanna blow that baby out of your back through your stomach. Truth be told, it would be better off dead than having you for a mother anyway," I said, chuckling without humor.

The way her eyes narrowed on my face told me that my words had finally shook her smug self-satisfaction, and that felt good to me. So, I kept pushing.

"You know, now that I think about it, I kinda understand why you wanted to have more kids, especially since you didn't raise your first one. And then, when you did finally decide to be a mother, she preferred her dad and me over you. That must have hurt your pride, Sha..."

"My daughter could NEVER love you more than me, bitch!" she growled, looking at me with hate and death in her eyes.

"Oh, really? Would you like to put that theory to the test?"

I could tell by the contortion of her face that my question was causing her some confusion, so I moved the gun from in front of my face and pulled my baklava off.

"Ty!" Dayjah exclaimed excitedly as her face lit up in the semi darkness.

She took a step toward me, but Shaomi put a quick stop to that by putting a hand to her ponytail and snatching her backwards.

"Ow! Mommy, that hurt," Dayjah said, pouting.

"Stay still and don't move until I tell you to," Shaomi said harshly.

"And the award for mommy of the year goes to..." I said sarcastically.

"Fuck you, bitch. I'm a better mother than you'll ever be, and once you die, I'll raise your little bastard to call me mommy too."

"Not if you're dead first," I said, raising the gun again and preparing to take the kill shot.

"Not today, bitch."

Suddenly, the power to the whole house went out, throwing everything, including the veranda, into complete darkness. I pulled the trigger twice, but I didn't dare swing the gun because I had no idea where the kids were, and I didn't want to hit them. I sidestepped in case Shaomi had a gun, and that way I was no longer where she last saw me. I could hear the children a few feet in front of me, but I could barely make out their silhouettes because the moon wasn't high enough yet. Sudden gunfire rang out from inside the house, and when I turned to look, all I saw were gun barrel flames shooting from the second floor. The lights snapped back on, and I looked behind me to where Shaomi had stood, but she was gone, along with Dayjah. The other kids were seated on the ground, calm, as if they'd been prepared for this somehow.

"Ms. Walker, we have to go. General Umar's army is coming fast," one of my men said.

In an instant, Shaomi's smug attitude made sense, as well as why she'd been so talkative. It was a trap, and I'd stepped into it, but it hadn't caught me yet. Which was why I had no choice but to run.

Chapter 14

(Royal)

The cold water thrown in my face woke me up, but the punch to my temple almost knocked me back out again. My vision swam like I was drowning in the Pacific and trying to see under miles of water to shore. I was still able to make out two men holding machine guns standing in front of me, and my first thought was about being able to slowly torture them both. I was able to see out of the window of the apartment that I was being held in, which told me that I was still inside the building that Ty had sought sanctuary in. The fact that my arms and legs were restrained by zip ties connected to bolts in the wall meant that I was definitely an unwanted guest. The apparent knowledge led to my next thought of the warning that Juan-Carlos had given me about this building being enemy territory. Maybe I should've listened, but it was too late for that now because I was obviously in the thick of things.

"Alright, listen, if you let me go now, I'll spare you later," I bargained, speaking Spanish to avoid being misunderstood.

Neither man said a word, but both of them wore a smirk that was quickly pissing me off.

"It's obvious that you two don't know who I am, so I suggest that you go get your boss before you do some shit that you can't get out of," I warned.

"La Jefa is coming," one man replied, smiling and showing me his bottom row of gold teeth.

The fact that his boss was a woman, based on how he addressed her, gave me a small piece of hope that I could talk my way out of this without too much effort. Women were innately more rational than men, maybe because there was no ego to deal with or because they tended to focus on the future and not just the present. Whatever the reasoning behind the decision making, I liked the odds of negotiating my freedom more now than I had a couple minutes ago. I chose not to say anything else to antagonize these foot soldiers and instead rehearsed what I would say to the woman in charge. A few minutes later, I heard a door open up to my left, around a corner that was out of my sight, and in my mind, that signaled game time. I saw the white sundress first, followed by her sexy, brown legs that led upwards to her enticing curves. Farther up my eyes traveled, admiring her beauty in silence, until I got to her face... And then, my heart stopped completely because her beauty was one that I remembered.

"All glory be to God for this gifted miracle that he has brought me. I have prayed to see your face again in this lifetime, in hopes that I would be given the opportunity to remove the light from your eyes the way that you did my son, Paco," Marta said, stopping right in front of me and looking up.

Her eyes were the same shade of black that I was now remembering from the night that David and I had run down on her home in Fort Lauderdale, Florida. They simply held more hatred now, and I knew that I'd put that there.

"It was just business, not personal," I said.

"Murder is always personal, especially when it comes to murdering one's familia," she replied.

In my mind, I was trying to understand how a Columbian born female could be leading a Mexican cartel, but the policies and nuances wouldn't save my life. The question was what WOULD save my life in this moment because, as far as I could see, it was going to take several superheroes.

"There isn't a day that goes by when I don't miss my Paco. His smile could melt my heart, even when I was mad at him about something, which was one of the things that him and his papi had in common. I understand that it was business for you all to kill my Viktor because he was a man who choose to live his life by the rules of the street. But killing Paco... and trying to kill me, that was savage. That was something that we didn't deserve," she said, pulling open the top of her dress to reveal two healed bullet wounds.

I didn't need to see them because I remembered vividly the moment that I'd decided to put them there. David had been of the mind frame to let Marta and Paco live, but I knew the danger in that because I knew that the thirst for revenge was insatiable. The only way to prevent it was to eliminate it, so that was the decision I'd made, and I would make it every time I was faced with that option.

"You call it savage of me, but is that not the world you're a part of too? Do cartels not kill entire families just to send a message?"

"Yes, but what message were you sending? At that time, you had no idea who I was, and you had already killed the man you came for. You could have showed mercy!" she said angrily, pointing the gun at my face.

I didn't say shit, choosing instead to say my prayers for God to watch over all the loved ones I was leaving behind. I was mentally prepared to die, but my heart hurt for my family that I was leaving, especially Tesha and Stormy. Most people that I knew, who would find themselves in this situation, would wish to undo what they did to get here, but I couldn't. I lived my life my way, so I stared at Marta and looked down the barrel of her gun without fear because all of this was my choice.

"I will show you mercy now, Marta, by warning you that I'm not a nigga that you wanna kill. I come from a powerful family that will not stop until they annihilate everything and everyone in this world that you care about if you kill me."

"Revenge is my only love now, thanks to you. Do not worry though because this will be a long love affair between you and I, and I can promise you that you will never get a bullet," she replied, lowering her gun.

She removed a straight razor from her bra, flicked it open, and stepped closer to me. When she put the blade on my left shoulder, our eyes locked, and then, she began to drag it slowly downwards, across my chest in a diagonal motion. I couldn't stop the scream that leapt from my throat as the skin beneath my shirt ripped open and immediately gushed blood. My entire body bucked against the restraints in a reflex motion, trying to get away from the razor's sharp edge, but there was nowhere to go. The gleam in her eyes spoke of the undeniable truth, which was that we both knew that I was stuck in the position that I would eventually die in. I knew that begging would change nothing, but reasoning might.

"My-My name is Royal Walker. Do your research before you do something that can't be taken back."

"I have more pressing matters to deal with, but I'll be back for you sooner than later. In the meantime, my men will keep you company," she replied, turning to address her soldiers.

In Spanish, she told them to hurt, but don't kill, me before she tucked her razor back into her cleavage and left. In the aftermath of her departure, her goons had a quick discussion about who was going to go first as they sat their guns in a corner of the room. I felt fortunate that the smaller guy won until I felt his first punch to my unguarded testicles. I immediately vomited all over myself as a wave of pain rolled through me like I'd never known before in my lifetime. I was so blinded by snot and tears that I couldn't even see the little Mexican anymore, but I felt his next punch, and it landed in the same place as the first. This time when I heaved from my gut to empty its contents, I felt my bowels loosen, and then, I had shit literally running down my leg. My plight made both men laugh, and as the bigger one moved toward me, I felt myself wishing for death to embrace me before any more pain could come. Before I could formulate the wish into a prayer, the big Mexican cocked back and punched me in the nuts as hard as he could. This time, the pain was too intense, and I was mercifully allowed to slip into unconsciousness. I had no concept of time to gauge how long I'd been out, but when I opened my eyes, I could tell by the fading twilight that significant time had passed. The smells of shit, piss, vomit, and blood filled my nostrils and made me gag hard enough to bounce my head off of the wall. As soon as that happened, I could hear movement from somewhere in the apartment, and then, my tormentors reappeared with plates of food in their hands. The aroma of Mexican cuisine was so far out of place that it could've been comical, but there wasn't a damn thing funny to me right now.

"Ten million. I'll give you ten million dollars if you let me go," I mumbled, hearing the rasp in my voice from my bruised vocal cords.

"Ten million pesos is not enough to betray Red Devil," the smaller man replied.

"Not-Not pesos. I'll give you ten million American dollars each. Tax free. All you have to do is get me out of here," I said.

Their clear understanding became evident by the fact that they stopped eating and looked at each other in silent communication. This gave me a small piece of hope.

"Ten million each? You have the kind of money?" the big man asked, stepping closer to me.

"Yeah, I do."

The wheels of decision making were turning fast behind his brown eyes, and I knew that he was seeing the life that only a cartel leader could imagine. My offer was speaking to his greed and his ambition because they were the things that made his loyalty for sale.

"I can get you any kind of product you want too. Good dope from Russia, Africa, or the U.S. because I've got connections everywhere," I said, trying to sweeten the offer beyond any resistance still lingering.

Before either man could answer, I heard the door to the apartment open again, and a few moments later, Marta walked in with two more soldiers trailing behind her.

"Smells like you've had an interesting afternoon, Mr. Walker, but it wasn't too much fun, huh?" she asked rhetorically.

"You know who I am, which means that you know why it's best to let me go without further harm."

"Let you go? Aren't you even gonna offer me the same twenty million and open-ended drug pipeline that you were promising my men?" she asked, feigning being wounded over not getting the same courtesy.

The two men that I'd made the offer to looked as shocked as I was feeling about her ability to repeat the conversation that we were just in the middle of having. That told me that they'd been unaware that we were being observed in some way the whole time. The two men that had walked in with her swiftly turned their guns on the other two men and executed them with double tap head shots. The bloody brain splatter on the walls locked like the work of a temperamental artist who only sold his work at high end galleries.

"As you can see, Mr. Walker, who you are and what meager things you have to offer are unimpressive to someone with equal or greater power than you. I do not fear you or your family, but I do understand how tempting it can be for someone who has never had more than their mama's tamale recipe. No worries though. I fixed those two before they became a problem, and I'm supremely confident in the new guards that I've chosen to keep you company. I've got business to tend to, but you boys play nice," she said, turning to leave.

"Marta, don't do this. It's not gonna bring Paco back, or anyone that you've loved and lost."

107

Her smile at my comment was cause for concern, even somehow enhancing her beauty.

"You never know, Mr. Walker. It might do the exact opposite of what you think. I guess only time will tell though, right? Soon, we'll see if you're the crown jewel in your father's crown or just another Royal in name only," she said, laughing as she walked out.

The men that she left to guard me this time had not an ounce of light behind their eyes, and I'd dealt with enough coldblooded killers to know what I was seeing in them. I waited for either of them to speak, but after a while, I saw that silence was their language of choice, which meant that it was up to me.

"Look, I don't know what the Red Devil told you, but me and my family are more powerful than anyone you've ever run up against. There's no way for you or your men to win a war against us, but I promise to spare you and your family if you let me walk out of here," I said.

I knew that Marta could still hear what I was saying through her listening devices, but I didn't give a fuck because I was dead regardless if I didn't try something. Neither man spoke. They just stood there, looking at me. They were both short and stocky, so in my mind, I named them Thing 1 and Thing 2 because they were an ugly set of twins.

"You want to walk out of here?" Thing 1 asked finally.

The way that he asked it, with a smirk on his face, told me that it was more than likely a trick of some sort involved, but I still nodded that I did want to walk out of here. He passed his gun to his man, pulled a box cutter out of his pocket, and came toward me. I didn't know what to expect, but he reached down and grabbed my leg where the zip tie was secured tightly. Hope swelled briefly, and then, without warning, he cut the bottom of my foot from heel to toe. I was still screaming in pain when I felt him do the same to my other foot, but then, I felt him cut all the zip ties loose, causing me to drop to the floor. Reflexively, I landed on my feet, but I immediately fell to my knees and inadvertently ran into the upper cut that Thing 1 was throwing my way with force. He connected solidly, sending me flying into the wall and putting me right back where I started. Unconscious.

Chapter 15

(David) (Ghana)

The flight from Mexico to Ghana was the tensest experience I'd ever had because everything in me wanted to either fly the plane or run faster than it. I'd hit my redial button so much that my fingers hurt, and my text messages weren't getting answered either. All in all, I felt completely powerless, and that wasn't a feeling that I enjoyed, so I filled my mind with the many different ways to kill Ty. By the time Carrie and I landed in Ghana, I'd decided on the idea of terrorizing every drop of blood out of my soon to be ex-wife's body, and then, I'd drink the blood nice and slow over some giant ice cubes.

"Let me guess. The hunter green Range Rover is yours," Carrie said as we got off of the plane in our private hangar.

"Don't judge me. Just shut up and get in."

"Oh, there's no judgement here, my king. I'm just admiring the luxurious life you ran off to while leaving your best friend behind," she said, smiling.

I ignored her guilt trip, hopped behind the wheel, and guided us out of the hangar.

"Try calling again," I said, pushing her my phone.

She took it and did as I asked, but the result was the same cycle of endless rings from my uncle and Shaomi's phones that had been received since midway through our flight. I had no idea what was going on, but my gut told me that it was all bad. It took us twenty minutes to arrive at my compound, and the amount of guards blocking the front gate was more alarming than reassuring. Guns immediately came up until I was recognized, and then, the sea of men quickly parted to let me through to where my uncle's second in command stood. General Udoku was a mountain of a man, standing at least 6'3", weighing at least two hundred eighty pounds easily, and he was fiercely loyal to my family. I could tell by the look on his face when I got out of the Range Rover that he was blaming himself for whatever bad news he had to deliver.

"General Udoku," I said.

"My king. I am sorry that I did not arrive sooner, but we mobilized as soon as Queen Shaomi activated the panic button in her bracelet."

"She ain't queen yet," Carrie mumbled under her breath as she came to stand beside me.

"What happened?" I asked.

"There was a sudden attack of the premises, and our people were overpowered. All of the guards were killed."

"And what of my uncle and Shaomi?" I asked, fearing the worst.

"Queen Shaomi, Prince David, and Princess Dayjah were able to escape and are awaiting your arrival in a secure location. Would you like to go to them now?"

"Where's my uncle?" I asked, not missing the fact that Udoku had said nothing of his fate.

The look on his face was saying plenty to me, and it wasn't good.

"We don't know the fate of General Umar right now, only that he was taken by whoever committed this act of war," Udoku replied.

I silently processed his words, trying to understand what Ty's play was by kidnapping my uncle in the country where he had the most power and influence. Was this her bargaining chip to try and stay alive, or was there more going on here?

IMMA DIE BOUT MINE 4 | ARYANNA

"Doesn't my uncle keep a tracker in him?"

"Yes, but it was cut out of his arm, and we found it discarded with his clothing by the side of the road not far from here," Udoku replied.

"I want every available soldier under your command out looking for my uncle, and their instructions are to kill whoever is holding him captive."

"David... Think about what you're saying," Carrie said, grabbing my hand so that I would look over at her.

"I know exactly what I'm saying. She attacked my home, where my kids are, and she kidnapped my uncle. She dies for that," I said unflinchingly.

"Okay, but just take a second and think all of this through. Tynesha is on the run with your kid, and she is obviously desperate, but where the fuck did she pick up the manpower to storm your compound? And in your backyard no less? Come on, David. Something about this shit sounds off, and you know it," Carrie stated.

"It's not off. You just don't want to admit the truth about how fucked up Ty has become. Obviously, she had help, and it was probably the fucking cartel who helped her traitorous ass," I replied, growing angrier by the second.

"So, your theory is that Tynesha, who's on the run for capital murder, convinced members of the Mexican Cartel to jump continents and start a war? With the most powerful muthafuckas on that continent? That makes sense to you?" Carrie asked, speaking slowly and clearly like I was a child.

Her tone alone served to piss me off even more, but my mind was really struggling with finding holes in her argument. I had no doubt that Ty had enough hate in her heart for me to want to see me dead, but she wasn't dumb enough to play her hand like this.

"General Udoku, what do you think?" I asked.

"I do not know, sire, but I know that the children said that the men who attacked this place were African, speaking a common African dialect. Not Mexican."

112

His revelation only added more mystery to what the fuck was actually going on, but I knew just the place to get answers.

"Take me to Shaomi," I demanded.

Udoku gave a curt nod before turning and leading the way toward the house. Carrie's hand stayed in mine as we followed him, and she occasionally gave my fingers a reassuring squeeze. Udoku led us through the main house, out onto the veranda, and then over to the wrought iron staircase that descended down the backside of my property to the desert floor. Once here, we came to an old shack that had been a secret hiding place of my father's that he'd built by hand when he was a boy. Since I'd taken up permanent residence here, I'd modernized it, and it had become a secret place where Shaomi and I hid from the world because few people knew about it. I wasn't surprised that it was her first choice of places to hide.

"Thank you, Udoku. I can take it from here," I said.

"Then I will see to finding your uncle as if it were my life's one mission. I will leave some of our best men to guard the compound."

I nodded, and he left without another word. As I headed for the door to the shack, Carrie let my hand go, even though she stayed in step with me, but I understood and appreciated her discretion. I made sure to open the door slowly so that I wouldn't startle anyone, and the first thing that I saw was Shaomi sitting on the only bed in the small, one room space. I could tell that Prince David was sleeping by the way that he was cradled in his mother's arms, but Dayjah's eyes spotted me, and she was wide awake.

"Daddy!" she screamed, scurrying off the bed and bolting into my arms.

I opened my arms wide and caught her out of midair, holding her close as she buried her face in my neck and cried.

"It's okay, baby. I know you're scared. I'm here though. Daddy is right here," I said, soothing her with my words as I gently rubbed her back.

Over Dayjah's shoulder, I could see Shaomi watching us until her eyes switched gears and looked past me. I could tell the moment that she spotted Carrie because the temperature dropped by at least twenty degrees with a storm's quickness.

"I see you brought company," Shaomi stated tightly.

"I just happened to be in the neighborhood, and I wanted to see this gorgeous little man that David told me about," Carrie said, moving past me and heading straight for Shaomi.

I felt like someone on the highway watching an accident in the making, and it would've been impossible for me to look away. Shaomi kept shit cute though and turned our son toward Carrie so that she could get a good look at him.

"Awww, he's so adorable! David, I want one," Carrie said, turning and looking back at me.

"Now ain't the time for jokes, bitch, so miss me with that dumb shit," Shaomi said, her tone deadly serious.

Carrie was still looking at me, so only I could see her smiling with mischievous intent, and I quickly shook my head at her.

"What?" Carrie asked, moving back toward me.

Part of me wanted to laugh, but I kept a straight face as I put my focus back on Shaomi.

"What happened, Sha?" I asked.

"Ty showed up shooting shit. That's what happened," she replied testily.

"Are you sure it was Ty?" Carrie asked.

"I think I know what the fuck my own cousin looks like, so if you don't have something constructive to say, then I suggest you keep your lips closed," she replied aggressively.

"Now see, I'm a real nice person, but that don't mean that fighting a pregnant bitch is beneath me," Carrie warned.

"Say what?" Shaomi asked, gently laying our son down on the bed.

"Ayo, both of you tighten the fuck up because we got bigger problems," I growled, trying not to raise my voice in front of Dayjah, who was still clinging to me.

"You better get her," Shaomi said, pointing a finger at Carrie.

"Been there, done that, and wore his muthafuckin T-shirt," Carrie replied sassily.

"Bitch, I know you lying because my nigga would NEVA fuck an albino."

Before Carrie could spill the tea, I turned to her and gave her ass a look that silenced her before I turned back to Shaomi.

"Tell me what Ty said. What was her plan?" I asked.

"The bitch didn't have a plan, David. She just came here to kill me. That's all. It's a good thing that your paranoia rubbed off on me, and I had my bracelet on to send for help."

"How did she get away then?" I asked.

"Before she made it to the main house, I set the timer to shut the main power off, knowing that the backup generator would sound another alarm in case my panic button failed. When the power went out, I grabbed Dayjah and ran down here."

'Mommy hurt me," Dayjah said softly against my neck.

"What happened, baby? How did Mommy hurt you?" I asked, holding her so that I could see her face.

"I didn't hurt her. She just don't know how to listen," Shaomi said defensively.

"She pulled my hair when I saw Mama Ty," Dayjah mumbled.

"Ty ain't your goddamn mama!" Shaomi said angrily, making a quick move toward us.

Before I could say or do anything, Carrie had stepped forward and squared up with Shaomi.

"I'll beat you until you miscarry if you take another step," Carrie vowed.

The sound of my phone ringing startled all of us, but I was more focused on stopping the potential fight that was about to start.

"Carrie, take Dayjah," I insisted, once again stepping in between her and Shaomi.

Carrie took her from my arms, allowing me to turn back around and face Shaomi.

"Why exactly did you pull our daughter's hair?" I asked.

"Because she was trying to run towards an obviously mentally fucked up woman with a gun in her hands. Was I not supposed to protect our child, nigga?"

The logic of her response was undeniable, so I didn't push the fight that I wanted to have.

"Did you see what went down with Umar before he was taken?" I asked.

"No, I was too busy making sure that me and your kids were safe. Sorry," she replied sarcastically.

I had more questions, but my phone had yet to stop ringing, which meant that someone was desperate to get in touch with me. When I finally pulled my phone out, I saw a number that I didn't recognize, but it was definitely from this continent, so I answered it.

"Who is this?" I asked.

"It's General Udoku, my king. I need you to come up to the front gate immediately please."

"I'm on my way," I replied, hanging up.

"What's up?" Carrie asked immediately.

"I don't know, but I'm being summoned to the front gate. Shaomi, you stay here with the kids, and Carrie, you come with me," I instructed.

I could tell by the look on Shaomi's face that she wanted to argue, but Carrie never gave her the chance because she handed her Dayjah and turned for the door.

"I'll call you when it's safe to bring them back to the main house," I said, passing her my phone and following Carrie out of the door.

"I don't like her anymore," Carrie said as soon as we began walking away.

"I couldn't tell."

My sarcasm caused her to give me a light shove as she laughed. We quickly made it back to the veranda, but before we headed out front, I led Carrie to my gun room so that we could strap up.

"Wow, David, this is a lot of firepower in here," she said, turning in a slow circle.

"You can never have too much. Shit turns you on, doesn't it?"

"Mmm hmm, my pussy is on slip and slide right now. Do we have time for a quickie?" she asked.

I didn't even need to look at her to know that she was serious, but I laughed it off as I grabbed a pistol.

"Stay focused and come on," I demanded.

She grabbed the twin to the Ruger .45 automatic I was clutching, and then, we headed back outside. There was no sound of a commotion, but there was definitely a crowd, and there were guns drawn.

"What's wrong, Udoku?" I asked, approaching with a little caution.

"An uninvited guest, my king. She claims to be your wife."

For a split second, I thought that he was being funny until he stepped back and brought me face to face with Tynesha.

"David, I need your help. It's-It's about our kids."

Chapter 16

(Tynesha)

"Why-Why should you spare me and my son? Because we have taken nothing from you. We were innocent in the war between Viktor and David," I replied.

"Somehow, I don't believe that you were as innocent in all of this as you would have me believe right now. Given how easily you killed the man that you've been sharing a bed with for the past year, it is obvious to me that you had blood on your hands long before now. Even the look in your eyes at this moment doesn't show the appropriate amount of fear, only calculation for your next move against me and my grandmother should we slip up. You would kill us both, right?"

"No," I replied, shaking my head emphatically.

"Really? Why not?"

Her question sounded dumb to me because we both knew that I was lying right now, which gave me the random thought that her question was a test instead. To what end, I didn't know yet.

"Killing you both wouldn't make good sense. It would only put a bigger target on my back. Assuming that me and my son even made it out of the building alive," I said, looking her squarely in the eyes.

"That is very logical thinking, and I like that about you because most cannot apply logic in high stress conversations or situations such as this. You give me extreme hope for the future."

"What does that mean exactly?" I asked, sensing something unexpected to come.

"Why don't you hand your nino over to my abuela so that we can talk more, without all of these guns of course?"

"I can talk to you just fine while I hold him," I replied.

Abuela was already moving in my direction, like she didn't just hear the words that came out of my goddamn mouth.

"No harm will come to him as long as you follow my instructions, so I will tell you one more time. Hand him over."

Her tone remained civil, but the flashes in her eyes were heat lightening warnings of a coming storm. The thought of grabbing my gun again occupied the frontal lobe of my mind, but I knew what I'd told her about not making it out of the building alive was a certainty. The only hope that me and my son had was playing the long game, and somehow, I knew that the Red Devil was counting on me to come to this conclusion. She wanted something from me. I just didn't know what yet. I waited a few more minutes for Rashon to finish his bottle, and then, I gently passed him off to Abuela. The sight of this 4'9", one hundred pounds grandma holding my son in one arm and her shotgun in her other would've been funny as fuck if it was someone else's kid. I had no reason to smile or laugh, so I turned my attention to Red Devil and waited for her to speak. She took a seat beside me on the couch, putting her gun on the coffee table where either of us could easily reach it, and then, she sat back with her legs crossed.

"I'm going to fill in whatever gaps you have about how you and your son came to this exact moment in time because that seems like the fair thing to do. For starters, my real name is Marta. I was born in a small town in Columbia and raised in Florida from the time I was fourteen, which was where I met Viktor Bah. I'll save you the boring love story, but he was a man that I loved very much despite the bad things that I knew he did. I was with him as he earned his way up in the Zoe Pound organization, and I watched him with pride even though I knew the inevitable consequences that came with his life. Those consequences became my reality on the night that your husband and our guest downstairs invaded my house."

"I'm not making excuses for what happened to you, but I know for a fact that David tried to have a peaceful sit down with Viktor Bah. Viktor shot him and almost killed him, which is what really started the all out war with Zoe Pound. On top of that, I got kidnapped by a Zoe Pound associate," I explained.

"I admit that I know nothing about what you are saying because I wasn't involved with Viktor's day to day business anymore. Once I had our son, my only goal in life was to be a good mother and to keep him away from the world's influence because I knew that it would call to him. It was in his DNA, given to him by me and Viktor. My Paco was a good boy though, and he would've become a great man were it not for Royal Walker."

"Royal?" I asked, surprised that this woman even knew his name.

"Yes, it was Royal who killed my Paco and shot me two times in the chest while leaving me to court death alongside him. Your husband, David... He wanted to spare me and Paco. He told Royal that we weren't a threat, but Royal ignored him, and I had to watch as he shot my innocent little boy in the head."

I took a moment to try and digest the many emotions that she, or any mother, would've had to feel as a result of this tragedy, but it was impossible to simulate. The thought of my child dying was like opening a black hole inside of me, and it was guaranteed to devour all things in its path. Now I understood the hatred that I'd seen in Marta's eyes, and I knew that there was nothing in this world, short of reincarnation, that could extinguish that flame. This knowledge put fear in me where none had existed before.

"Since I know that you don't have David downstairs, are you trying to tell me that you have Royal?" I asked.

"Precisely, and I owe that to you."

"Wait, so you're saying that Royal was in Mexico City looking for me and my son?" I asked, making sure that I was comprehending fully.

"Si. He showed up at the front desk, but the fact that he had no idea where he was suggested to my people that something was off about him. So, they notified my men, and the rest is history in the making."

Her explanation sounded simple enough, but my mind was still on the fact that Royal was in Mexico City looking for me and mine. For him to know where I was meant that he probably knew what I'd done, but there was no way that this was a rescue mission. Royal was head over heels in love with Tesha, and the last thing that I'd promised my twin was to kill her and the baby she'd had by my husband. There was absolutely no way that she would send her nigga to help me, which meant that he had other motivations for tracking me down. He'd come to kill me and my son.

"What are you going to do to Royal? I mean, I'm sure that you've heard of his family," I said.

"Yes, I know who they are. They made a lot of noise in the U.S. and then in Brazil a few years after that, but I'm not worried about them. They're gonna be my friends, just like you are," she replied, smiling brightly.

"How's that gonna work?"

"It's really simple on both parts. For Royal's family, well, they have the power, resources, and they're crazy enough to break the first man that I ever loved out of prison. That will help replace the life that Royal took when he killed Viktor. And your part, well, all you have to do is bring me a child that is worth the life of your child," she said nonchalantly.

"What the fuck do you mean that I have to bring you a child worth the life of my child?" I asked with barely controlled rage calling for me to grab a gun and shoot this bitch.

"I lost a child, so someone else must lose one too. If you don't want that child to be yours, then you must bring me one that is either Royal's or has Royal's blood. If you do that, then I will give you your son back, and you both will be free to go, but if you don't, then you'll be left to always wonder what became of your son."

Her words rang in a way that was haunting, and it tapped into a recent memory that I'd been desperately trying to forget for months now. I studied her face, looking for any signs of a bluff, but there were none because this lady wasn't bullshitting in the slightest. Now, I fully understood why this had to be the long game, even though I needed to figure out what I was going to do and how I was going to play it asap.

"How do you expect me to get close enough to Royal's family to kidnap a child? Contrary to what he told you, he's no friend of mine, and I suspect that he was here to kill me on orders from his girlfriend, who just happens to be my sister."

A look of delight and amusement covered her face, and I had to resist the real urge to smack flames from her muthafuckin ass.

"You make me wish that we had more time together to gossip and share the disturbing tales of our dysfunctional families, but maybe another day. I'm not unsympathetic to your plight, so I'll adjust my demands just this once. If you can't capture a child near and dear to Royal, then you must kill one and bring me proof. If you try any of those T.V. Hollywood tricks, I promise that I'll kill your son while you watch, and then, you die next. Understand?" she asked.

"Yeah, I got it."

"Good. Now, where would you like my men to drop you?" she asked, picking up her pistol and rising to her feet.

I stood up, once again contemplating fucking this bitch up and killing her, but I knew that wasn't my play right now. I would wait, but the woman before me was dead, even if she didn't know it yet.

"I need to get to the nearest airport," I replied.

"I don't think that flying commercially is your best option because, if you get locked up, then you'll definitely lose your son forever. Luckily for you, I've got a plane and a pilot, so where are you going?"

"Africa," I replied without hesitation.

Her eyebrow shot up in a quizzical way, but I didn't offer up any explanation. It was obvious to me that she knew who Royal and his family were, but she didn't know about David and his family. That ignorance could work to our advantage if I could convince David not to kill me as soon as he saw me.

"Come with me," she instructed, leading me out of the apartment into the hallway.

Once there, she gave instructions to the two men guarding the door to her penthouse to see to it that I got to the airfield outside the city. Without a word, they began walking away, and I was forced to fall into step behind them. The sound of my heart shattering grew louder the farther away I moved from Rashon, and by the time I made it to the elevator, I was using the wall to keep me from crumbling. The thought of leaving my son behind had hot bile rolling through my stomach like a ride at an amusement park, and for a few seconds, all I saw was stars swimming in my vision. It took all of my strength not to pass out, but I finally overcame the urge and stepped onto the elevator.

For the entire ride down, I put my focus on numbing myself from the inside out because I knew that there was no other way I was going to mentally survive what was next to come. I wasn't willing to give up my son, which meant that I would do anything that I had to do in order to avoid that pain. By the time that I climbed into the back of the Dodge

TRX truck for the ride to the airfield, I'd tucked my weakness into the darkest part of myself, and my focus was on the task ahead. It took us forty-five minutes to get to the field where a small, two prop engine plane awaited, but the pilot wasted no time getting me in the air. He let me know that the flight to Ghana would take a few hours, but the problem was that he had nowhere to land because this wasn't a scheduled flight. I thought about what could be done to fix this issue without me having to produce my passport to customs because that would be more than a huge gamble, and Marta's words about the consequences of prison weren't forgotten either.

It wasn't until we were almost there that I had a wild ass idea pop into my mind, causing me to pull my phone out. I boldly contacted the main airport in Ghana and told them that King David Bishop's wife was en route and required a car and driver waiting on the tarmac. Per their protocol, I was told that a representative would meet me on the ground to verify my identity so that I could avoid the crowds. After I hung up, I prayed extra hard that David hadn't changed his security protocols to exclude me, but even if he had, this would still work out.

Worst case scenario was that they detained me until he got here, and then, I would plead my case to him. Even using this logic, I was still a nervous fucking wreck when I got off the plane, especially because I still had all of my guns in my possession, including the one I'd used to kill Roland. As soon as my feet touched the pavement, there was a tall, stern looking, Black man with some type of handheld scanner in his grip. When he thrust it at me, I said another silent prayer, and then, I laid my right palm on it. Within seconds, my name and face popped up, and everything was flowing green arrows.

"Your car is this way, my queen," the man said, sidestepping so that I could move toward the green Mercedes S700.

My movements could've been attributed to any woman who knew that this was her station in life, even though my nerves were beyond frayed, and my mouth was bitter with the taste of fear. I said not a word until I was comfortably seated in the back of the car, and then, I told the driver to take me home. It was a quick twenty minutes later when the car came to a stop at the entrance to the compound, and all I could see through the window was armed military guards. The way that they all aimed their guns at the car told me that this was more than heightened security measures. Something had happened. I slowly got out of the car, keeping my hands high and visible, but that didn't lower the temperature at all.

"State your business here."

"I'm King David's lawful wife, married to him by General Umar himself," I replied.

Murmurs swiftly moved through the crowd, but I kept my eyes on a man who said nothing as he pulled out a phone. It was a long ten minutes later before I heard David's voice, and then, I was pulled forward through the crowd until I was face to face with him.

"David, I need your help. It's-It's about our kids," I blurted emotionally.

Chapter 17

(Tesha) (Nigeria)

The entire trip back to Nigeria, I'd been stone silent, fuming over the fact that I'd allowed that snake ass bitch the chance to play me. Instead of listening to her, I should've been knocking her goddamn brains out of her skull with my AR-15 bullets, but I'd been caught up in getting closure. I'd lost focus, just for a second, and that shot had almost gotten me and the men who'd gone with me killed. I felt like a fucking failure, and I couldn't even bring myself to call Royal and tell him how badly I'd fucked up. I knew that he'd still love me, and he'd tell me that it wasn't that bad, but that was not what I wanted to hear because it WAS that bad! The element of surprise was a crucial thing in any war, and my mistake had cost us that at the very least. There was no way to undo that mistake, and not even the consolation prize of kidnapping General Umar could make up for it. The whole trip, I'd been trying to figure out how best to utilize Umar, but so far, all I'd come up with was a trade scenario where David had to give up Shaomi or watch his uncle die. After everything that had happened, I wouldn't rest until Shaomi was dead, and I knew that just as sure as I knew my daughter's name. When the plane finally touched down on the private airfield that Royal had inside his compound, my mind was buzzing with ideas on how to kill Shaomi, but the moment that I saw Royal's sisters come out of the house, I blanked out. I couldn't keep a single thought in my head except that something was all the way the fuck wrong. I hit the ground on the run as soon as the plane stopped rolling, heading straight toward my in-laws and silently praying the whole way.

"What is it? What's wrong? Where's Royal?" I asked in rapid fire succession.

"Tesha, breathe," Free said.

"I'm breathing!" I shrieked, losing the battle with my tears as they poured from my eyes.

Angel stepped forward and put her hands on both of my shoulders.

"Take deep breaths, sweetie. Don't try to talk, just breathe," she instructed.

It took everything in me to follow her instructions, but with each deep breath I took, the knowledge that something was wrong continued to burrow deeper into my brain. I tried to keep my focus on Angel's face because I felt like I was about to pass the fuck out at any second. After a few moments of breathing slowly, my heart finally stopped pounding loud enough to drown out a marching band, and I felt some of my composure return. Whatever happened, I knew that I needed a clear head to make my way through it.

"Okay, tell me," I said in a calmer tone.

\"Something went wrong in Mexico, and we think that Royal was betrayed by someone in the Juarez cartel. He sent a message saying that a nigga named Juan-Carlos had left him outside of the building that he'd tracked your sister's last movements to. We haven't heard from him since," Angel said.

"Did you track the GPS on his phone?" I asked.

"I did, but there's something powerful blocking his signal. The last reading that I got was right outside of that building in Mexico City," Destiny replied.

"Who owns the building?" I asked.

"Shell corporations with ties to Mexico and Columbia, so most likely, it's a rival cartel. We don't know for sure, but if

Roland was working with the Zeta Cartel and Ty was able to get help from a cartel in Mexico, then the odds are good that it's them," Destiny said.

I processed this information rapidly, already searching my mind for the most logical plan of attack. The wrong move could have catastrophic consequences, and if that in any way involved Royal losing his life, then it was unacceptable.

"How long has it been?" I asked.

"A few hours, but we believe that he's alive in that building somewhere," Free replied.

"Based on what?" I asked, looking for some hope to hold onto.

"The first thing that Royal would've done was make it clear who he is, and who his family is, in order to either bribe or intimidate whoever has him. If he was dead, we'd know that already," Angel said.

"Destiny, can't you pull up whatever cameras they have? If Royal tracked Ty to that building, then that means there has to be images of her," I reasoned.

"Those were my thoughts exactly, but whoever owns that building must have figured out how Royal tracked Ty that far too because the camera system for that entire block has been pulled offline. We can't see shit," Destiny replied, clearly frustrated.

This news only succeeded in adding another knot to the spider web in my stomach, but I didn't lose my composure again because there wasn't any time for that. I needed to think clearly because that was what Royal would tell me to do, and that was how we would bring him home safely.

"So, we go to Mexico and knock the goddamn building down if we have to," I said seriously.

"Spoken like a true Walker," Angel said, giving my shoulders a gentle squeeze before she took a step back.

"Royal has three buildings on this property the size of large warehouses, full of weapons and armored vehicles," I said.

"For what?" Free asked, surprised.

"For whatever war is coming next. He told me that he knew your family's retirement would only last for so long, which was why he'd been secretly buying everything that the black market has to offer in the realm of military materials," I replied.

"So, when doomsday comes, my little brother didn't build a bunker like normal people. He built a fucking war chest?" Angel asked, shaking her head with a rueful smile.

"He's definitely his daddy's son," Destiny said.

"Speaking of which, have any of you spoken to FatherGod yet?" I asked, looking from one woman to the other.

The guilty expression that all of them wore was answer enough, but we all knew that it was inevitable.

"We can't do this without his knowledge because the ramifications are too big. We've gotta let him know at least," I insisted.

"We're all in agreement on that part, but we can't go to Dad without all the facts because he'll fuck us up for that," Destiny stated.

"What happened in Ghana?" Free asked, switching subjects.

I shook my head, still disgusted with myself, but determined to put it behind me.

"I fucked up, and Shaomi got away. I shouldn't have hesitated, but she told me that she was pregnant again, plus she was surrounded by little kids, and I..."

"We get it. It's never easy to shoot in that situation. Do you know if your plan to lure David back to Ghana worked?" Free asked.

"Oh, yeah, he's definitely back by now and probably sitting by the phone waiting on me to call," I replied, smirking.

"Okay, uh, why would he be waiting on you to contact him or call?" Angel asked, looking at me closely.

"Well, because I abducted his uncle, who happens to be one of the most powerful and feared men in all of Africa."

They shared a look that I couldn't decipher, and then, they burst into unexpected laughter.

"Bitch, I know you lying," Destiny said.

"No cap. That nigga is in the plane unconscious, bound and gagged," I replied, pointing over my shoulder.

"Okay, so what's your plan for him?" Free asked seriously.

"I don't know yet, but I know that he's leverage, and being he's the leader of an army out here, I think we can use it to my advantage," I said.

"Now you've got my mind working," Free admitted, looking past me toward the plane.

For a moment, we all paused and simply waited as we watched her mentally chewing on something that had the creases on her forehead protruding.

"We can use David's uncle to make David join forces with us to help secure Royal's release. It gives us even more power, and we may need it," Free said.

"You really think that a Mexican cartel has the juice to stand up to whatever we're bringing?" Angel asked, looking at Free.

"You gotta remember that we ain't a gang; we're a family. We have the means to buy people's loyalty, but we'd be fools to think that we're the only ones using that tactic of manipulation. I'm not running through this in my mind like we're just going after one cartel. I'm of the mind to anticipate an eventual showdown between us and La Eme," Free replied.

"La Eme? As in the Mexican Mafia?" Destiny asked.

"The one and only. I know what you're gonna say, and yeah, we have some connections with them because of Dad, but this is different. This is us attacking their people, and I'm not convinced that this is something that they'll stand down for. Mexicans are proud people, and I have no doubt that we're gonna seem like the bully to them, even if this was a fight that they started by fucking with Royal," Free replied. We all listened to her words and contemplated the ramifications in silence. I had no doubt that each and every one of us was willing to die for Royal, but we knew that going about this the smart way increased the odds of survival. I couldn't see raising Stormy without Royal right there by my side, so I'd do whatever, and align myself with whoever, in order to get my husband back.

"Okay, so Destiny, we need more info on which exact cartel owns that building and who runs that organization. Free and Angel, will you help me interrogate General Umar?" I asked.

"Lead the way," Free replied.

Destiny headed back inside the main house, which was a fourteen-bedroom mansion, while we headed back out into the field where the plane sat. By now, Royal's men had pulled Umar out of the cargo hold, and they had him laid out, still bound and gagged on the grass while they stood over him.

"Get him up," I demanded, stopping a few feet away.

When they pulled him to his feet, I could tell that he had regained consciousness, and the fire in his eyes indicated that he was none too happy with my treatment of him.

"This is a chance to prove your usefulness to us, or you can die right here in this field," I said, roughly pulling the gag out of his mouth.

"Such tough talk from a little girl," he replied, flexing his jaw to loosen it up.

"We're not little girls though, and we damn sure don't have a problem slumping you," Free stated, pulling her two-tone Glock .27 out and chambering the first round.

Umar's eyes shifted to Free, and he stared at her in silence for a moment before turning his attention back on me.

"I know who you and your sisters are, but this has nothing to do with you," he said.

"On the contrary. Tesha is our sister too because she's married to our little brother, and that means that this has everything to do with us," Angel said, pulling out her own gun and cocking it.

I could instantly see Umar's facial expression shift as he made the business decision not to piss off my sisters.

"What do you want?" he asked.

"What do you know about Mexican cartels?" I asked.

His smirk felt like he was calling me stupid, so I stepped forward and threw a fast jab that landed squarely on his nose.

"Next time, I'mma hit you with the butt of my gun again," I threatened.

He took a few moments to shake off the aftereffects of his eyes watering, but when he refocused on me, I could see his desire for violence clearly.

"I know a lot about the cartels, and I do business with the Sinola cartel," he replied.

"We used to do business with the Juarez Cartel, but we got betrayed. The question that I have is if we attack the cartel, will the Mexican Mafia get involved?" Free asked.

"Guaranteed," he replied without hesitation.

'In that case, we need you and your men to help level the playing field," I said.

"And why would I do that? Why would I help the woman who killed some of my men and kidnapped me?"

"Because a war is coming, and you're smart enough to be on the right side of it. This fight involves all of us because the cartel is notorious for targeting families, and in case you've forgotten, my daughter is still David's child," I stated.

"How do you think your people would view you if they knew that you let an heir to the throne get slaughtered?" Free asked logically.

His look of resignation said it all, but I still felt like he needed more convincing.

"If you really don't wanna help, Uncle Umar, I could always retaliate against the cartel in your name and honor, which guarantees that you and your people become targets. The price on your head would continue to rise until some brave soul put your head in a box and mailed it back to Mexico. I could make it look like a mutiny of your army and negotiate our peace that way. It's more complicated but just as effective in ending a war that no one really wants. What do you think?" I asked innocently.

Angel let out a long whistle and patted me on the back.

"Well played," Free said, nodding, impressed at my improv job.

Umar was far from amused, but he was also nobody's fool. One way or another, him and his army were going to fight, but he could do it his way or mine.

"I will not make this decision without David. I cannot. He is king on the throne, and his word is law. So, if you want my army's help, then it's him that you must convince," Umar stated.

I felt like all of us wanted to call bullshit on what he was saying, but the fact that it made sense kept us quiet.

"Okay, I'll call him," I said, pulling my phone out.

I quickly scrolled through my missed calls until I found his number, and then, I hit the send button. After five rings, it was answered.

"Who is this?" a familiar female voice asked.

"It's Tesha, and I need to talk to David. Now."

Chapter 18

(David)

The gun in my hand came up of its own volition, and before I knew it, I had the barrel of the .45 pressed to Ty's skull. I was definitely looking to give her another hole to breathe through.

"Where is my uncle?" I demanded, growling the words through my clenched jaw.

"Y-Your uncle? Why would I know where your uncle is? I came to talk about..."

"Bitch, don't play dumb with me because I know exactly why you came! You made a fatal mistake if you thought that you could negotiate with my uncle's life in person because I'll splatter your shit if you don't tell me where the fuck he is," I vowed, giving the trigger under my finger a gentle caress.

"David, listen to me. I don't know where your goddamn uncle is! Your son is in danger though, and I need..."

"Hold up, hold up. Tynesha, did you or did you not just storm this place with some hired hittas a few hours ago and kidnap David's uncle?" Carrie asked, stepping up beside me.

"What? No. Fuck no! Why would I kidnap Umar? I love him like my own uncle," Ty proclaimed.

The shock on her face looked genuine, but I knew just how convincingly she could lie.

"Last chance and I ain't bout to ask again. Where is my uncle?" I asked, cocking the hammer on my pistol.

"D-David, I swear on the lives of our children that I didn't have anything to do with your uncle's kidnapping. Why would I come back here if I kidnapped him?"

"David, wait, she's got a point," Carrie said, putting her hand on my arm gently.

I wanted to pull the trigger so bad that I felt like I could taste gunpowder on my tongue, but deep down, I knew that I was tapping into the steady reserve of hate that I felt for this woman. In my mind, she deserved to die, but I needed to know where my uncle was first.

"If I think you're lying, you're dead before the thought can leave your deceitful tongue," I warned.

"Fair enough. Now, tell us what happened, and why did you say that David's kids were in danger?" Carrie asked, gently pulling my arm away from Ty's head as she calmly stepped in between us.

"Our-Our son, Rashon, has been kidnapped by the head of the Zeta Cartel, and I need David's help to get him back."

"This is your fault then because he probably got kidnapped for some fuck shit that your nigga, Roland, did!" I replied heatedly.

"No, nigga, it was some fuck shit that you did!" she yelled, trying to get past Carrie like she wanted to swing at me.

"Ty, chill! What are you talking about?" Carrie asked, refusing to let her past.

"The head of the cartel is a woman named Marta, and she was the mistress of..."

"Viktor Bah," I said, suddenly feeling sick to my stomach.

"Wait, is she talking about Fort Lauderdale?" Carrie asked, looking over her shoulder at me.

I nodded, but my brain was still trying to comprehend what Ty had said because it didn't make sense.

"Marta is dead though. Royal shot her and her son, Paco," I murmured, reliving that fateful night in my mind.

"Are you saying that they survived?" Carrie asked, looking back at Ty.

"Not they... just Marta. Viktor and Paco are dead, and Marta is now ready to destroy our world in the name of revenge. She has our son, and she has unreasonable demands in order for us to get him back," Ty said, crying silent tears as her eyes continued to fill with hopelessness.

"What does she want?" I asked, feeling suddenly dizzy like I'd been kicked by a mule.

"She-She wants someone that she loves broken out of prison, and she wants a life equal to Rashon's life. More specifically, she wants Royal's child or a child that Royal loves," Ty replied, looking up at me.

'So, she-she wants me to choose between my children? How the fuck am I supposed to do that?" I asked hollowly, taking several steps backwards while letting my pistol slide from my grip.

I put my hands to my head in hopes of easing the increasing pressure that was building up, but the thumping continued. I felt a hand on my forearm, and I looked down, expecting to see Carrie, but instead, I found Ty right in front of me.

"I'm so incredibly sorry for everything that I put you through, and one day, I hope that we can sit down to hash all of that out. Right now, I need you to help me save our kids," she said softly.

"I don't know how to fix this," I admitted, feeling the first tears making tracks down my face.

"We'll figure it out, and we'll do it without losing Rashon or Stormy. We all love your kids, David," Carrie said, stepping up beside Ty and putting her hand on my other arm.

"There's something else that you need to know first," Ty said.

The change in her tone made me look at her closer because I could sense the distress. Despite everything that had happened between her and I, I still felt like I knew her better than anyone else in the world did.

"What is it?" I asked.

"I-I gave birth to twins."

I felt my mouth go slack immediately, and I could feel my tongue slap my chin in a comical way.

"Wait, what? Bitch, you had twins?" Carrie asked.

"There was no report of that, and only one DNA sample was run for comparison," I said.

"How did you know about... So, those results were your doing?" Ty asked, cocking her head to the side.

"Uncle Umar did it to protect you and Rashon because he figured that you weren't the one who ran the test," I replied, thinking back to the last full conversation I'd had with my uncle.

His wisdom was still unparalleled.

"Uh, can you two stay focused please? Where's this twin at?" Carrie asked.

"Honestly, I don't know. I had to give her away before Roland found out, so I never even got to hold my baby girl," Ty replied, choking back more tears of pain.

"David! David, your phone! It was Tesha who..."

I turned at the sound of Shaomi's voice, and I was surprised to see her a few feet from us with my phone in one hand and a pistol in the other. Before I could ask a question, I saw Shaomi's eyes skate past me in Ty's direction, and then, the gun in her hand came up.

"No!" I yelled, stepping in front of Ty, but there was already smoke wafting from the gun's barrel. The bullet caught me smack in the middle of my chest and lifted me off of my feet. I felt Ty absorb my weight as we both went to the ground, and when I looked up, I saw Shaomi advancing on us. Before she could take two steps, I saw Carrie's hand swing up, and the pistol in her grip barked loudly twice, knocking Shaomi down instantly. Ty's face loomed over mine, and her beauty made me smile. I took one shuddering breath that hurt beyond any description of pain I knew, forcing me to close my eyes. And then, I felt nothing...

To be continued...

Coming Soon
I'MMA DIE BOUT MINE 5

Lock Down Publications and Ca$h Presents
Assisted Publishing Packages

BASIC PACKAGE $499 Editing Cover Design Formatting	**UPGRADED PACKAGE** $800 Typing Editing Cover Design Formatting
ADVANCE PACKAGE $1,200 Typing Editing Cover Design Formatting Copyright registration Proofreading Upload book to Amazon	**LDP SUPREME PACKAGE** $1,500 Typing Editing Cover Design Formatting Copyright registration Proofreading Set up Amazon account Upload book to Amazon Advertise on LDP, Amazon and Facebook Page

***Other services available upon request.
Additional charges may apply

Lock Down Publications
P.O. Box 944
Stockbridge, GA 30281-9998
Phone: 470 303-9761

Submission Guideline

Submit the first three chapters of your completed manuscript to ldpsubmissions@gmail.com. In the subject line add **Your Book's Title**. The manuscript must be in a Word Doc file and sent as an attachment. Document should be in Times New Roman, double spaced, and in size 12 font. Also, provide your synopsis and full contact information. If sending multiple submissions, they must each be in a separate email.

Have a story but no way to send it electronically? You can still submit to LDP/Ca$h Presents. Send in the first three chapters, written or typed, of your completed manuscript to:

LDP: Submissions Dept
P.O. Box 944
Stockbridge, GA 30281-9998

DO NOT send original manuscript. Must be a duplicate.
Provide your synopsis and a cover letter containing your full contact information.

Thanks for considering LDP and Ca$h Presents.

NEW RELEASES

BLOODLINE OF A SAVAGE 1&2
THESE VICIOUS STREETS
RELENTLESS GOON
RELENTLESS GOON 2
BY PRINCE A. TAUHID

THE BUTTERFLY MAFIA 1-3
BY FUMIYA PAYNE

A THUG'S STREET PRINCESS 1&2
BY MEESHA

CITY OF SMOKE 2
BY MOLOTTI

STEPPERS 1,2&3
BY KING RIO

THE LANE 1&2
BY KEN-KEN SPENCE

THUG OF SPADES 1&2
LOVE IN THE TRENCHES 2
BY COREY ROBINSON

TIL DEATH 3
BY ARYANNA

THE BIRTH OF A GANGSTER 4
BY DELMONT PLAYER

PRODUCT OF THE STREETS 1&2
BY DEMOND "MONEY" ANDERSON

NO TIME FOR ERROR
BY KEESE

MONEY HUNGRY DEMONS
BY TRANAY ADAMS

Coming Soon from Lock Down Publications/Ca$h Presents

IF YOU CROSS ME ONCE 6
ANGEL V
By Anthony Fields

IMMA DIE BOUT MINE 4&5
By Aryanna

A THUGS STREET PRINCESS 3
By Meesha

PRODUCT OF THE STREETS 3
By Demond Money Anderson

CORNER BOYS
By Corey Robinson

SON OF A DOPE FIEND 4
By Renta

THE MURDER QUEENS 6&7
By Michael Gallon

CITY OF SMOKE 3
By Molotti

BETRAYAL OF A G
By Ray Vinci

CONFESSIONS OF A DOPE BOY
By Nicholas Lock

143

THA TAKEOVER
By Keith Chandler

Available Now

RESTRAINING ORDER 1 & 2
By **CA$H & Coffee**

LOVE KNOWS NO BOUNDARIES 1-3
By **Coffee**

RAISED AS A GOON I, II, III & IV
BRED BY THE SLUMS I, II, III
BLAST FOR ME I & II
ROTTEN TO THE CORE I II III
A BRONX TALE I, II, III
DUFFLE BAG CARTEL I II III IV V VI
HEARTLESS GOON I II III IV V
A SAVAGE DOPEBOY I II
DRUG LORDS I II III
CUTTHROAT MAFIA I II
KING OF THE TRENCHES
By **Ghost**

LAY IT DOWN I & II
LAST OF A DYING BREED I II
BLOOD STAINS OF A SHOTTA I & II III
By **Jamaica**

LOYAL TO THE GAME I II III
LIFE OF SIN I, II III
By **TJ & Jelissa**

IF LOVING HIM IS WRONG…I & II
LOVE ME EVEN WHEN IT HURTS I II III
By **Jelissa**

IMMA DIE BOUT MINE 4 | ARYANNA

BLOODY COMMAS I & II
SKI MASK CARTEL I, II & III
KING OF NEW YORK I II, III IV V
RISE TO POWER I II III
COKE KINGS I II III IV V
BORN HEARTLESS I II III IV
KING OF THE TRAP I II
By **T.J. Edwards**

WHEN THE STREETS CLAP BACK I & II III
THE HEART OF A SAVAGE I II III IV
MONEY MAFIA I II
LOYAL TO THE SOIL I II III
By **Jibril Williams**

A DISTINGUISHED THUG STOLE MY HEART I II &
III
LOVE SHOULDN'T HURT I II III IV
RENEGADE BOYS 1-4
PAID IN KARMA 1-3
SAVAGE STORMS 1-3
AN UNFORESEEN LOVE 1-3
BABY, I'M WINTERTIME COLD 1-3
A THUG'S STREET PRINCESS 1&2
By **Meesha**

A GANGSTER'S CODE 1-3
A GANGSTER'S SYN 1-3
THE SAVAGE LIFE 1-3
CHAINED TO THE STREETS 1-3
BLOOD ON THE MONEY 1-3
A GANGSTA'S PAIN 1-3
BEAUTIFUL LIES AND UGLY TRUTHS
CHURCH IN THESE STREETS
By **J-Blunt**

PUSH IT TO THE LIMIT
By **Bre' Hayes**

BLOOD OF A BOSS 1-5
SHADOWS OF THE GAME
TRAP BASTARD
By **Askari**

THE STREETS BLEED MURDER 1-3
THE HEART OF A GANGSTA 1-3
By **Jerry Jackson**

CUM FOR ME 1-8
An LDP Erotica Collaboration

BRIDE OF A HUSTLA 1-3
THE FETTI GIRLS 1-3
CORRUPTED BY A GANGSTA 1-4
BLINDED BY HIS LOVE
THE PRICE YOU PAY FOR LOVE 1-3
DOPE GIRL MAGIC 1-3
By **Destiny Skai**

WHEN A GOOD GIRL GOES BAD
By **Adrienne**

A KINGPIN'S AMBITION
A KINGPIN'S AMBITION II
I MURDER FOR THE DOUGH
By **Ambitious**

THE COST OF LOYALTY 1-3
By **Kweli**

IMMA DIE BOUT MINE 4 | ARYANNA

A GANGSTER'S REVENGE 1-4
THE BOSS MAN'S DAUGHTERS 1-5
A SAVAGE LOVE 1&2
BAE BELONGS TO ME 1&2
A HUSTLER'S DECEIT 1-3
WHAT BAD BITCHES DO 1-3
SOUL OF A MONSTER 1-3
KILL ZONE
A DOPE BOY'S QUEEN 1-3
TIL DEATH 1-3
IMMA DIE BOUT MINE 1-3
By **Aryanna**

TRUE SAVAGE 1-7
DOPE BOY MAGIC 1-3
MIDNIGHT CARTEL 1-3
CITY OF KINGZ 1&2
NIGHTMARE ON SILENT AVE
THE PLUG OF LIL MEXICO 1&2
CLASSIC CITY
By **Chris Green**

A DOPEBOY'S PRAYER
By **Eddie "Wolf" Lee**

THE KING CARTEL 1-3
By **Frank Gresham**

THESE NIGGAS AIN'T LOYAL 1-3
By **Nikki Tee**

GANGSTA SHYT 1-3
By **CATO**

THE ULTIMATE BETRAYAL
By **Phoenix**

BOSS'N UP 1-3
By **Royal Nicole**

I LOVE YOU TO DEATH
By **Destiny J**

I RIDE FOR MY HITTA
I STILL RIDE FOR MY HITTA
By **Misty Holt**

LOVE & CHASIN' PAPER
By **Qay Crockett**

TO DIE IN VAIN
SINS OF A HUSTLA
By **ASAD**

BROOKLYN HUSTLAZ
By **Boogsy Morina**

BROOKLYN ON LOCK 1 & 2
By **Sonovia**

GANGSTA CITY
By **Teddy Duke**

A DRUG KING AND HIS DIAMOND 1-3
A DOPEMAN'S RICHES
HER MAN, MINE'S TOO 1&2
CASH MONEY HO'S
THE WIFEY I USED TO BE 1&2
PRETTY GIRLS DO NASTY THINGS
By **Nicole Goosby**

LIPSTICK KILLAH 1-3
CRIME OF PASSION 1-3
FRIEND OR FOE 1-3
By **Mimi**

TRAPHOUSE KING 1-3
KINGPIN KILLAZ 1-3
STREET KINGS 1&2
PAID IN BLOOD 1&2
CARTEL KILLAZ 1-3
DOPE GODS 1&2
By **Hood Rich**

STEADY MOBBN' 1-3
THE STREETS STAINED MY SOUL 1-3
By **Marcellus Allen**

WHO SHOT YA 1-3
SON OF A DOPE FIEND 1-3
HEAVEN GOT A GHETTO 1&2
SKI MASK MONEY 1&2
By **Renta**

GORILLAZ IN THE BAY 1-4
TEARS OF A GANGSTA 1/&2
3X KRAZY 1&2
STRAIGHT BEAST MODE 1&2
By **DE'KARI**

TRIGGADALE 1-3
MURDA WAS THE CASE 1-3
By **Elijah R. Freeman**

THE STREETS ARE CALLING
By **Duquie Wilson**

SLAUGHTER GANG 1-3
RUTHLESS HEART 1-3
By **Willie Slaughter**

GOD BLESS THE TRAPPERS 1-3
THESE SCANDALOUS STREETS 1-3
FEAR MY GANGSTA 1-5
THESE STREETS DON'T LOVE NOBODY 1-2
BURY ME A G 1-5
A GANGSTA'S EMPIRE 1-4
THE DOPEMAN'S BODYGAURD 1&2
THE REALEST KILLAZ 1-3
THE LAST OF THE OGS 1-3
By **Tranay Adams**

MARRIED TO A BOSS 1-3
By **Destiny Skai & Chris Green**

KINGZ OF THE GAME 1-7
CRIME BOSS 1-3
By **Playa Ray**

FUK SHYT
By **Blakk Diamond**

DON'T F#CK WITH MY HEART 1&2
By **Linnea**

ADDICTED TO THE DRAMA 1-3
IN THE ARM OF HIS BOSS
By **Jamila**

LOYALTY AIN'T PROMISED 1&2
By **Keith Williams**

YAYO 1-4
A SHOOTER'S AMBITION 1&2
BRED IN THE GAME
By **S. Allen**

TRAP GOD 1-3
RICH $AVAGE 1-3
MONEY IN THE GRAVE 1-3
CARTEL MONEY
By **Martell Troublesome Bolden**

FOREVER GANGSTA 1&2
GLOCKS ON SATIN SHEETS 1&2
By **Adrian Dulan**

TOE TAGZ 1-4
LEVELS TO THIS SHYT 1&2
IT'S JUST ME AND YOU
By **Ah'Million**

KINGPIN DREAMS 1-3
RAN OFF ON DA PLUG
By **Paper Boi Rari**

CONFESSIONS OF A GANGSTA 1-4
CONFESSIONS OF A JACKBOY 1-3
CONFESSIONS OF A HITMAN
By **Nicholas Lock**

I'M NOTHING WITHOUT HIS LOVE
SINS OF A THUG
TO THE THUG I LOVED BEFORE
A GANGSTA SAVED XMAS
IN A HUSTLER I TRUST
By **Monet Dragun**

QUIET MONEY 1-3
THUG LIFE 1-3
EXTENDED CLIP 1&2
A GANGSTA'S PARADISE
By **Trai'Quan**

CAUGHT UP IN THE LIFE 1-3
THE STREETS NEVER LET GO 1-3
By **Robert Baptiste**

NEW TO THE GAME 1-3
MONEY, MURDER & MEMORIES 1-3
By **Malik D. Rice**

CREAM 2-3
THE STREETS WILL TALK
By **Yolanda Moore**

LIFE OF A SAVAGE 1-4
A GANGSTA'S QUR'AN 1-4
MURDA SEASON 1-3
GANGLAND CARTEL 1-3
CHI'RAQ GANGSTAS 1-4
KILLERS ON ELM STREET 1-3
JACK BOYZ N DA BRONX 1-3
A DOPEBOY'S DREAM 1-3
JACK BOYS VS DOPE BOYS 1-3
COKE GIRLZ
COKE BOYS
SOSA GANG 1&2
BRONX SAVAGES
BODYMORE KINGPINS
BLOOD OF A GOON
By **Romell Tukes**

IMMA DIE BOUT MINE 4 | ARYANNA

THE STREETS MADE ME 1-3
By **Larry D. Wright**

CONCRETE KILLA 1-3
VICIOUS LOYALTY 1-3
By **Kingpen**

THE ULTIMATE SACRIFICE 1-6
KHADIFI
IF YOU CROSS ME ONCE 1-3
ANGEL 1-4
IN THE BLINK OF AN EYE
By **Anthony Fields**

THE LIFE OF A HOOD STAR
By **Ca$h & Rashia Wilson**

THE STREETS WILL NEVER CLOSE 1-3
By **K'ajji**

NIGHTMARES OF A HUSTLA 1-3
By **King Dream**

HARD AND RUTHLESS 1&2
MOB TOWN 251
THE BILLIONAIRE BENTLEYS 1-3
REAL G'S MOVE IN SILENCE
By **Von Diesel**

GHOST MOB
By **Stilloan Robinson**

MOB TIES 1-6
SOUL OF A HUSTLER, HEART OF A KILLER 1-3
GORILLAZ IN THE TRENCHES
By **SayNoMore**

BODYMORE MURDERLAND 1-3
THE BIRTH OF A GANGSTER 1-4
By **Delmont Player**

FOR THE LOVE OF A BOSS 1&2
By **C. D. Blue**

KILLA KOUNTY 1-5
By **Khufu**

MOBBED UP 1-4
THE BRICK MAN 1-5
THE COCAINE PRINCESS 1-10
STEPPERS 1-3
SUPER GREMLIN 1-4
By **King Rio**

MONEY GAME 1&2
By **Smoove Dolla**

A GANGSTA'S KARMA 1-4
By **FLAME**

KING OF THE TRENCHES 1-3
By **GHOST & TRANAY ADAMS**

QUEEN OF THE ZOO 1&2
By **Black Migo**

GRIMEY WAYS 1-3
By **Ray Vinci**

XMAS WITH AN ATL SHOOTER
By **Ca$h & Destiny Skai**

IMMA DIE BOUT MINE 4 | ARYANNA

KING KILLA 1&2
By **Vincent "Vitto" Holloway**

BETRAYAL OF A THUG 1&2
By **Fre$h**

THE MURDER QUEENS 1-5
By **Michael Gallon**

FOR THE LOVE OF BLOOD 1-4
By **Jamel Mitchell**

HOOD CONSIGLIERE 1&2
NO TIME FOR ERROR
By **Keese**

PROTÉGÉ OF A LEGEND 1&2
LOVE IN THE TRENCHES 1&2
By **Corey Robinson**

BORN IN THE GRAVE 1-3
CRIME PAYS
By **Self Made Tay**

MOAN IN MY MOUTH
By **XTASY**

TORN BETWEEN A GANGSTER AND A GENTLEMAN
By **J-BLUNT & Miss Kim**

LOYALTY IS EVERYTHING 1-3
CITY OF SMOKE 1&2
By **Molotti**

HERE TODAY GONE TOMORROW 1&2
By **Fly Rock**

WOMEN LIE MEN LIE 1-4
FIFTY SHADES OF SNOW 1-3
STACK BEFORE YOU SPLURGE
GIRLS FALL LIKE DOMINOES
NAÏVE TO THE STREETS
By **ROY MILLIGAN**

PILLOW PRINCESS
By **S. Hawkins**

THE BUTTERFLY MAFIA 1-3
SALUTE MY SAVAGERY 1&2
By **Fumiya Payne**

THE LANE 1&2
By Ken-Ken Spence

THE PUSSY TRAP 1-5
By **Nene Capri**

DIRTY DNA
By **Blaque**

SANCTIFIED AND HORNY
by **XTASY**

BOOKS BY LDP'S CEO, CA$H

TRUST IN NO MAN
TRUST IN NO MAN 2
TRUST IN NO MAN 3
BONDED BY BLOOD
SHORTY GOT A THUG
THUGS CRY
THUGS CRY 2
THUGS CRY 3
TRUST NO BITCH
TRUST NO BITCH 2
TRUST NO BITCH 3
TIL MY CASKET DROPS
RESTRAINING ORDER
RESTRAINING ORDER 2
IN LOVE WITH A CONVICT
LIFE OF A HOOD STAR
XMAS WITH AN ATL SHOOTER

www.ingramcontent.com/pod-product-compliance
Lightning Source LLC
Chambersburg PA
CBHW060421260626
47161CB00005B/1731